Stories You Won't Believe

by

Lonnie E. Brown

STORIES YOU WON'T BELIEVE

Published by Winchester Cottage Print

In Louisville, KY

Printed by LSI, Nashville, TN

U.S.A.

Cover and design by Jill Baker

Illustrated by Jill Baker

Printed in the United States of America

Copyright 2017

DEDICATION

This book is dedicated to my wife, Roberta Simpson Brown, who made this book possible by nagging me to write and by typing the manuscript.

It is also dedicated to my late parents, Lucian E. and Lena Mae Brown, who told me stories and allowed me to explore life on my own. And to my brothers and sisters, Neline, Lewis, El Wanda, Del Vontrice, and H. L. (known as Charlie), and their families, especially Charles Kerr, Pattie Filley, Billy Hurt, and Vicki Brown.

It is dedicated also to my best friend through the years, Jerry Anderson, who was with me in all my explorations and adventures, helping me carry them out.

And last, I dedicate this to all my boyhood friends (Hollis DeHart, Roger Hopper, Joseph Miller, A. G. Reese, and Ronald Smith); to my current golfing buddies, (partner Grover Gaddie, and all the members of the Mel Forman League); and to all my musicians friends I had the pleasure of playing music with through the years.

-----Lonnie E. Brown

ACKNOWLEDGMENTS

The number of people who helped bring this collection together is too large to list by individual names. I would like to name a few, however.

Thanks to Jill Baker, renowned artist and publisher, for the cover, illustrations and for the publication of this revised book.

I am grateful to my entire family named in the dedication and all my wife's family for all their support: my mother-in-law (Lillian Simpson) and my father-in-law (Tom Simpson) who told me many stories while breaking green beans; my sister-in-law (Fatima) and her husband (Ervin Atchley) who always encouraged me in my music.

I especially thank special friends who have given me endless encouragement, fun, and support: Sharon Brown; Heather Dotson; Vivian Duke; John and Carol Ferguson; Thomas Freese; Grover and Linda Gaddie; Dennis and Deanna Hansen and their family; Wanda Hargrove; Dolores Jackson; Marie Stewart; Norma Lewis (who laughs at all my funny sayings); Robert Parker (Mr. Ghost Walker, who shares special investigations with us); Lee and Joy Pennington; Joan Todd, and all the many friends we have that I don't have room to name.

I want to acknowledge how much the late Jennifer Smith meant to my wife and me. She was a beautiful lady with a beautiful spirit. She lived life fully with an upbeat, caring, and courageous attitude, and inspired others around her to do the same. She filled our lives with joy and goodness that remain even though she is gone. Here's to you, Jennifer, until we meet again!

STORIES YOU WON'T BELIEVE

Table of Contents

Illustrations by Jill Baker:

Stories You Won't Believe

by
Lonnie E. Brown

On hot days, the older folks would move to a shady spot on the front porch or under a tree.

Introduction

I come from a family and a community of storytellers. For a long time, I took that for granted. I did not realize what treasures these stories from these great storytellers really were. Now I go to festivals and pay admission to hear professional tellers do the same things these master tellers did for free.

My wife, friends, and associates kept pointing out that I had stories that should not be lost to future generations. I gave their comments some thought through the years, and I finally decided to put my stories together in a collection. This is the result. I hope you enjoy them and pass them on.

--Lonnie E. Brown

Granny and the Preacher

In my Grandmother Sally's day, Sundays on the family farm in central Kentucky were usually uneventful. We went to church, came home, ate dinner, and just sat around relaxing. Nothing exciting ever happened. That was about to change the day the preacher came for Sunday dinner.

Having the preacher over for Sunday dinner wasn't an unusual practice in itself. He took turns visiting members of his congregation each Sunday. His presence was considered an honor at the noon meal, so the women spared no effort to see that a feast would be waiting for the preacher after the Sunday service. That meant that at least one member of the family would stay home and have the food ready when the church service ended.

Grandmother Sally, a young teenager then, volunteered to stay behind on this particular

Sunday while the rest of the family went to hear the sermon and escort the preacher back with them for dinner.

Young Sally knew exactly what kind of meal the preacher expected. She put on a kettle of green beans, cut off a skillet of fresh corn to fry, and boiled potatoes for mashing. She killed, cut up, and fried three chickens to be sure there would be enough to satisfy all appetites. It was rumored that the preacher had been known to gobble up one entire chicken by himself. She baked cornbread, sliced onions and tomatoes, and set the homemade blackberry cobbler she'd made for dessert on the table to cool. Certain that everything was under control, she began cleaning up the kitchen.

She took the chicken entrails (intestines and other internal organs not edible) out behind the house and threw them down over the hill. Then she set the table and took up the food in bowls and platters. Since there were no screens on the doors and windows, she spread white tablecloths over the food to keep the flies off. She even chased the cats out, so they would not be tempted to sample the food. Then she stood looking out the door for the family and the preacher to arrive from church.

Sally didn't have to wait long. The preacher, dressed in the same old black suit he wore every Sunday, shook Sally's hand and followed the family into the main room where guests were entertained. He was offered the best chair the family owned

The preacher always tried to give the impression that he was a very humble man, so he began to protest.

"No! No!" he insisted. "This one is good enough for me. I'll sit right here."

The chair he chose was an old cane bottom chair that had a hole worn in the bottom from years of use. He pulled it near the fireplace where Sally had cooked her kettle of beans, and he sat talking to our family in a booming voice. He wriggled around in his old, threadbare suit as he gave his captive audience his second sermon of the day.

As young Sally listened, something dangling under the bottom of the chair caught her eye. She couldn't see clearly what it was, but something was definitely sticking through the hole in that old cane bottom chair.

Immediately, my young granny was mortified!

"Oh, Lord!" Sally said to herself. "Those hateful cats have dragged those chicken entrails in and left them in that chair, and the preacher has sat on them! If he sees them, we'll never be able to set foot in church again!"

As she frantically tried to think of what to do, she spied the poker propped up by the fireplace. She decided she would take the poker, jab the coals a couple of times like she was stirring the fire, and then casually reach under the chair with the poker and hook the chicken entrails while no one was watching.

Granny put her plan into action without any more thought. Nobody noticed as she eased up to the fireplace behind the preacher and stirred the fire. Nobody saw her as she slowly moved the poker under the chair. Then she made her hook!

The quiet Sunday visit was shattered by the preacher's shrieking as he leaped into the air. The cane bottom chair fell backward on Sally and the poker went flying from her hand to the side of the fireplace. The preacher did a holy dance holding his crotch, and Sally got her first view of a part of a man's anatomy that young unmarried girls did not see in those days.

The stunned family sat speechless as the preacher raced out the door. The ripped, threadbare pants clearly showed what innocent Sally had mistaken for chicken entrails.

My family changed churches after that, but they heard that the preacher gave up those Sunday dinners and went out and bought himself a brand new suit!

When Granny Was a Blushing Bride

Through the ages, brides have worried about the worst thing that could happen to them on their wedding day. My Grandmother Sally was no exception. Like all brides, she was concerned with her gown and food for her friends and relatives who would be attending her wedding at the little church near her home. Little did she know that these things would turn out to be the least of her worries.

On this sunny Saturday afternoon in the late 1800s, many people had already gathered in the two-story log cabin where Sally lived. They had come to wish her well and to accompany the wedding party to the church.

Her brother Howard and his friends sat in the large living room, looking out at the cornfield that bordered the front yard. They commented on the waist high corn in straight rows that had been hoed clean of weeds. The cleared middle between each row reminded them of the church aisle Sally would soon walk down.

While they talked, Sally climbed the steps to the upstairs bedroom to dress for her wedding. The floor consisted of loose 18-inch yellow poplar boards that Sally had crossed many times without mishap.

"Hurry, Sal!" Howard called up to her. "Ma says it's almost time to go."

Feeling pressured to hurry, Sal stripped off all her clothes and reached for her new white bloomers and petticoat beside the wedding gown. She did not notice that her mother had accidentally moved the bed a few inches from its usual place when she laid out the clothes. Completely unaware that one leg of the bed now rested on the edge of a loose board, Sally sat on the bed to pull on her bloomers. Her weight caused the board to flip, leaving a wide opening in the floor. Sally was horror stricken as the bed tilted and flung her down among the people below. There she lay, not in her wedding gown, but in her birthday suit!

When the stunned onlookers realized what had happened, they began to roar with laughter. Absolutely mortified, Sally struggled to her feet and dashed out the front door for cover in the cornfield. The cleared row did not offer her the protection she sought. Howard and his friends could clearly see her streaking down the cornrow directly in front of the doorway.

Attempting to direct her out of view, Howard yelled, "Skip a row, Sal! Skip a row!"

When Howard's words finally registered in the mind of the blushing bride-to-be, she skipped out of sight into the next row of corn.

By the time Sally's mother rescued her and escorted her to church, the groom, the preacher, and the guests were all waiting. If Sally blushed behind her veil, nobody noticed. They were all too busy trying not to laugh at the image engraved in their minds of Sally running naked down the corn row. She marched down the aisle without a worry in the world. The worst had already happened.

Most brides get only one new name on their wedding day, but my grandmother Sally acquired two. Her marriage gave her the title of Mrs. William Brown, but her friends gave her the nickname of Skip-A-Row-Sal!

Skipping School

Cornfields were common hiding places in the country. Like Grandmother Sally, I had headed there a few times myself to escape from an unpleasant situation. The time that stands out most clearly in my mind was the day my baby brother was born.

If you were a teen or a pre-teen in those days, the arrival of a new baby in the family was something of an embarrassment. You just didn't like to think that your parents had created another being! Besides, I had one brother and three sisters, and I figured enough was enough. Our parents informed us, however, that we would soon be having a new addition to the family.

He arrived one night late in February. Babies were born at home back then as a rule, so we weren't surprised when the midwife arrived after supper to help Mom with the delivery. Doctors were only called in if the birth was a particularly difficult one. We kids were sent to bed early and we slept through the birthing commotion.

Dad woke us for breakfast and told us we had a little baby brother. He also told us to get dressed, eat breakfast, and go to school. None of the things he said thrilled us except the part about eating breakfast.

"Come look at your new brother," Mom called from her bed.

My two youngest sisters, who were not yet old enough to go to school, ran over smiling to take a look. My brother, my other sister, and I remained at the table eating.

"Go on," Dad instructed.

We went about midway across the room, glanced at the bundle beside Mom, shrugged, put on our coats, hats, and gloves, grabbed our books and our lunches, and ran out the door for school.

"Another little crying baby," my younger brother said.

"Yeah," I agreed. "He'll keep us up all night squalling!"

"We'll all have more chores to do with Mom in bed for the next few days," my sister added.

I hadn't thought of that, but I knew she was right. I remembered that it had been that way when our two little sisters were born.

As we walked down the country road with these dreary thoughts in mind, we were definitely not this baby boy's best welcoming committee.

Just as we came to Amos Smith's house, his dogs raced out, barking furiously and nipping at our heels like they did at every opportunity. Usually, we picked up a stick before we approached the house so we could scare them off, but this morning we forgot, thanks to that baby. We took off running and escaped into the cornfield by the side of the road. The dogs lost interest and went back into their yard.

"Nothing's going right this morning," my sister said. "We've ended up in a cornfield."

"It would serve everybody right if we just stayed in the cornfield," I said.

"You know," said my sister, "that's not a bad idea. We should just skip school and stay here all day! Let 'um wonder what happened to us."

"Yeah," I agreed. "The kids will tease us all day if we go to school. Let's stay here! Then they'll be sorry!"

"I'm cold," complained my brother. It was a warm day for February, but it was still too cold for comfort. "I don't want to stay in a cornfield all day! We'll get in trouble!"

"Well, you're going to stay," my sister told him.

"I'm going to tell Dad that you made me stay," he replied, with the slightest whine in his voice.

"You tell and we'll beat your bottom," I threatened.

He settled down and reconciled himself to his plight for the time being, but it didn't last long. We were beginning to think we might have made a mistake because the February chill was already getting to our bones.

"What are we going to do all day?" he asked.

"Our school work," my sister answered.

We opened our books, sat on some fodder that was piled on the ground in one row, and worked on math and spelling. When my brother got bored, we made a game of it. Sometimes we stood up and ran around to get warm.

"I'm hungry!" my brother said. We opened our lunches and ate our bologna and cheese sandwiches.

"I'm thirsty! What have we got to drink?" my brother asked.

We usually drank water with our lunch at school, so, of course, we hadn't brought any with us.

"We can't drink until we get home," my sister told him.

That didn't make him happy at all.

"I'm going to tell on you when I get home," he muttered again, but a threatening look from me shut him up.

Time dragged on after we ate. I don't think any of us ever spent such a miserable day or a longer day in our lives. We didn't have a watch, so we didn't know what time school would be out. Finally we thought we heard the school bus bringing the kids home from the school in Russell

Springs. We figured our little country school must be out, too, so we decided it would be safe to go home. As soon as we entered the door, we knew we were wrong.

"What are you doing home early?" Dad wanted to know.

Before we could collect our thoughts and come up with a good excuse, our brother blurted out, "We didn't go to school today! We stayed in the cornfield!"

"You did what?" Dad asked.

My brother, in safe territory now, gave Dad all the details.

Mom was furious.

"You little devilish things!" she said. "If I could get out of this bed right now, I'd whip every one of you!"

Dad evidently thought we'd been punished enough by our own foolish actions, so he just talked to us instead of resorting to spanking. In the end, we certainly saw the error of our ways and promised never to do a thing like that again.

I think it was our embarrassment about our new brother that bothered Mom most of all.

"Don't you love the little fellow?" she asked, pulling the blanket back so we could see him better.

This time, we all moved up to the bedside. He was kicking his little feet and seemed to be looking around to see what kind of family he'd been born into. We all had to agree that he was sort of cute.

Day by day, he grew on us. Now we wouldn't trade him for all the cornfields on the planet!

We wouldn't trade the cornfield experience either. It made us feel a lot closer to Grandmother Sally because we all shared a common hiding place!

Uncle Buck Raises the Dead

My Grandmother Sally wasn't the only one to be involved in funny escapades. My grandfather Rooks, whom everybody called Uncle Buck when he was grown, had his own comical episodes.

Once when he was a boy in Adair County, Kentucky, my grandfather-to-be had to accompany his family to a wake. A wake was a gathering of relatives, friends, and neighbors to stay awake all night with the family of someone who had died. There were no funeral homes, so the deceased was kept at home for visitation until time for the funeral. Ladies would bring food, and men would sometimes bring something to drink. The corpse laid in bed while the men made his coffin. It was not only a sad time, but also a time for celebrating the life of the deceased.

This time, the deceased was a man in the community that everybody called Old Man

Campbell. He had spent his life raising sheep. In fact, he was one of the few to do so. He loved his sheep and always tended them with care, making sure they had food, water, shelter, and salt. But now, all that was over. His heart had given out.

When young Buck arrived with his family for the wake, the old log house was full of neighbors who had come to mourn and pay their respects to the family. The corpse had been washed, dressed, and laid out on the bed by the window since his coffin was still in the process of being constructed out in the barn. One by one, everybody filed by the bed to say their goodbyes before moving on around the large room to mingle with others who were there.

There weren't any children his age for company, so young Buck soon got bored among all those grownups. Since nobody was paying any attention to him, he decided he'd slip outside and find something interesting to do. The moon was full, so he had plenty of light to see.

At first, he didn't see anything that caught his fancy. As his gaze went beyond the yard, he saw something that caught his attention. He spied a long rail propped against the rail fence that surrounded the sheep pen. There was something about the angle of the rail that reminded him of a seesaw. Now that had possibilities! He looked around to find a place where he could set up the seesaw and make it work.

He was about to give up, when he noticed a chink had fallen out under the window of Mr. Campbell's old log house. He figured that if he slid one end of the rail into that chink between the logs, he could have a good time bouncing on the end of the rail that would be left sticking out.

He didn't hesitate to put his plan into action. He immediately took the rail from the fence and carried it to the side of the old log house. With little effort, he pushed it through the opening between the logs. Then he jumped on the end he'd left sticking out, happily bouncing up and down.

His happiness was short lived. To his amazement, he heard screams begin inside the house. Before he could dismount, people came pouring out of the house, some climbing out windows, others running out the door. Some stopped and stood there gasping, while others kept on running and didn't even look back. He sat on the rail thinking that the house must have caught on fire, until he felt his mother's hand clamp on his shoulder.

"Just what do you think you are doing, young man?" she asked, pulling him off the rail to the ground. "What did you mean by putting that rail through there? You scared us all half to death!"

Only then, looking into his mother's scowling face, did he realize what had happened. The window where he had placed the rail was directly beside the bed where the corpse was laid out. The rail that he had inserted in the opening had actually extended under the bed where Mr. Campbell rested, waiting for his coffin!

When young Buck had jumped on the end of the rail outside, the end of the rail under the bed inside went up, causing poor old dead Mr. Campbell suddenly to rise up in a sitting position and seem to come to life.

"Lord A-Mighty!" said Jesse Green, a neighbor who had been standing beside the bed. "Old Man Campbell has come back from the dead to salt his sheep!"

Nobody waited to see if that were true! Screaming to the top of their lungs, they scattered in all directions.

Buck tried to explain, but his mother was in no mood to listen. She took him back inside and he had to sit quietly with her and the few adults who had recovered from their fright and stayed behind. Together, they placed Mr. Campbell on the bed in a resting position again. And at future wakes, Uncle Buck's mother made sure he was never again out of her sight long enough to raise the dead.

Sheepish Buck

Since young Buck Rooks couldn't raise the dead anymore, he decided he wanted to raise a sheep. Old Man Campbell's family was selling some of his sheep after his death, so Buck's father bought him a good size lamb.

Buck spent much of his time caring for and playing with his new pet. There weren't many boys his age in the immediate area to offer companionship, so the sheep gave Buck many hours of recreation.

The neighbors on the next farm did have one son, Jim Will, but the boy wasn't too bright. He was a real thorn in Buck's side, following him around all the time asking what Buck thought were silly questions. If Buck tried to make Jim Will go away, Buck's mother would pull him aside and tell him his behavior was shameful.

"That poor boy can't help the way he is," she would remind Buck over and over. "It won't hurt you to play with him."

"But, Momma!" Buck would protest. "He's too slow-minded to catch on to games."

"Don't you hurt his feelings by saying things like that," she'd tell Buck. "Just be glad that you've got the sense God gave you!"

Buck's good sense was soon to be questioned.

Not long after Buck got his sheep, he began to get tired of their daily routine. He got the idea one day that it might be fun to build a little wagon and let the sheep pull him around the farm. When he asked his parents if he could build a little wagon, they thought it sounded like a constructive project. In their wildest imagination, they could not predict how it would end.

His dad gave him some popular lumber that was stacked in the barn, and Buck began to build a sturdy little wooden wagon big enough for him to ride in. As soon as he finished, he fashioned a little harness for the sheep. At last, he was ready to put his plan into action

On the day Buck was to make his test run with his sheep and little wagon, Jim Will and his mother came over to pay a visit. Buck was aggravated when he saw them coming. Jim Will would be underfoot while he made his final preparations. He tried to stay out of sight, but Jim Will came running to the barn.

"Can I ride, Buck? Can I?" Jim Will asked over and over.

"Okay," Buck finally agreed, "but I'm going to ride first."

"Aw! I want to ride now!" Jim Will persisted.

"No," Buck answered, standing his ground. "Me first!"

"Can't I do something?" asked Jim Will, not giving up.

Buck stood looking from his sheep to his little wagon and an idea popped into his head.

"Tell you what I'll do," he said to Jim Will. "To make it easier on my sheep, I'll hitch you to the wagon, too. You all can pull me. Then I'll hitch myself up to the wagon, and we'll pull you."

"Okay!" exclaimed Jim Will, jumping up and down.

Buck placed the harness he'd made on the sheep. Then he hastily fashioned a harness out of rope to use on Jim Will. In a short time, Jim Will and the sheep were hooked side by side in front of the wagon. Then Buck climbed in the wagon for what he thought would be a slow, pleasant ride across the field toward the springhouse.

"Git up, there," Buck called out, pulling on the reins.

"GIT UP," Jim Will yelled loudly, jumping up and down beside the sheep.

The sudden movement surprised and scared the sheep. Instead of moving forward in a slow walk, the sheep lurched forward and took off in a full run, dragging Jim Will along. The boy tried to get his balance, but the sheep was too fast for him. He was stumbling, falling, grunting, and holding on for dear life.

The run-away wagon threw Buck on his back with his feet in the air. The reins went flying out of his hands. As he struggled to get in an upright position, the sheep maintained its heading down toward the springhouse in Sulfur Creek!

Buck finally managed to sit up and grab the reins.

"Whoa!" he yelled. "Whoa!"

But the word wasn't in the sheep's vocabulary, or else it didn't hear. On it went down the hill at breakneck speed, bleating and bumping the wagon and poor Jim Will on the uneven ground.

Buck, holding on for dear life, still bounced on the bottom of the wagon and bumped against the sides.

By now, Buck was screaming at the sheep and Jim Will was sobbing from the bumps and scratches he was receiving as he was dragged along. The two mothers heard the commotion and ran outside just in time to see the out-of-control ride come to an abrupt and unhappy end.

The sheep had swerved to miss a head-on collision with a tree growing on the creek bank, but the wagon broadsided the tree and brought everything to a halt. Buck flew from the wagon and landed with a splash in the creek, knocking the family's supply of milk and butter from the spring box where it had been cooling for supper. Buck looked at it floating in the now muddy water and knew it couldn't be salvaged.

As Buck tried to shake the water from his drenched clothes, he tried to assess the damage the tree had done to his wagon, his sheep, and Jim Will. All were standing, so Buck felt a spark of hope that everything would be all right.

Buck's mother pulled him from the creek, while Jim Will's mother checked out her scratched and bleeding son. Now that he had a closer view, Buck could tell from Jim Will's crooked arm that he had obviously broken a bone. Buck knew he'd be lucky if his mother didn't break his neck. As her look of concern turned to anger, he knew he was in for it!

"What on earth possessed you to do such a thing?" she demanded to know! "You could have killed Jim Will."

Later, a sheepish looking Buck tried to explain what happened as his father unharnessed the sheep and helped Buck pull the wagon back to the barn.

Jim Will's broken bone mended and Buck's wagon was permanently retired from use.

The sheep never quite trusted Buck again. It showed remarkably good judgment in always keeping a safe distance. I guess it was afraid that if it ever got involved in one of Buck's escapades again, it might end up as lamb chops.

A Match for Me

There must have been genes in the male members of our family, which caused us to play pranks that got us in trouble. I suspected this when I was about nine years old and was forced into a situation against my will. Sometimes when cornered, boys, like skunks, will take action that may not make them a popular match with everybody around them.

It was a warm day in late spring, and I thought it would be a perfect time to go by my friend Jerry's house and persuade him to go swimming. I know it was Monday because Monday was washday in the country. The sun was just up, but my mom and older sister Neline were sorting the dirty clothes to get the wash done and on the line in time to dry. I had carried water from the spring and was just getting ready to make my get-away to Jerry's house when I heard a familiar voice from the front yard.

"Lena! It's me! Laurie! Where are you?"

"Here in the back," Mom called. "Come on around."

Aunt Laurie Sinclair came round the corner of the house, wearing her bonnet and apron and carrying an empty bucket.

"Oh, are you washing?" asked Aunt Laurie. "I already got my clothes hung out. Of course, I don't have many things to wash, living by myself and all."

"Yes, I do have several more to wash for," Mom answered.

"I was hoping you'd go sallet picking with me," said Aunt Laurie. "I've been wanting me a good mess of wild greens, but I don't like to go by myself. Snakes are out this time of year and a person could get bit."

"I'd like to go," Mom told her, "but I've already got my wash water on heating. I really have to get the washing done in time to dry. It may rain by late afternoon."

"Maybe Neline could go then," suggested Aunt Laurie.

"I need her to watch the little ones while I wash," Mom explained. "I wish I could help you out, but I can't today."

It was at that point that I made my first mistake of the day. I came out the back door and started across the yard to head to Jerry's house.

I felt Aunt Laurie's eyes focus on me. I should have dashed off and not looked back, but I froze like a deer in headlights.

"Lonnie could go with me, couldn't he?" Aunt Laurie asked.

"Why, yes!" Mom said. "I won't be needing him for a while."

All my senses came to life at once. I ran up to Mom pleading.

"Mom, don't make me go sallet picking! Jerry and I are going swimming this morning!"

"You and Jerry can swim anytime. Now go help your Aunt Laurie!" Mom ordered.

"But Mom!" I protested.

"Hush and go on before I get a switch to you," Mom insisted.

I knew I was no match for the two of them, so I reluctantly followed Aunt Laurie down the dirt road to Mr. Othie Brock's field by the branch. A barbed wire fence surrounded the field, but Aunt Laurie opened the narrow gate and held it while I went through. Then she carefully closed and fastened it behind us. Then she started walking through the tall sagebrush toward the little branch that flowed through the field.

"You can help me look for wild greens and we'll pick enough for your mom to fix, too," said Aunt Laurie.

I was still sullen from being forced to abandon my swimming plans, so I didn't answer. I wandered off by myself and pretended to look for poke, dandelion, dock, mustard and the like. Aunt Laurie had her back to me, bent over picking the wild greens she had located. The dry sagebrush rubbed against my leg as I walked with my hands in my pockets, and I stopped and looked at it. Then I made my second mistake for the day—so big, in fact, that it could have cost us our lives.

As I stood looking at the dry sagebrush, my fingers touched one of the treasures that boys my age always kept on hand. When Mom or one of the neighbors would send me to the store to get a box of matches, I always took out two or three and kept them in my pocket. They never missed them, but I had built up an ample supply for whatever I might need them for in the future. Today seemed like a good time to use one of them. If I could get this little area of sagebrush on fire, it would scare Aunt Laurie out of the field and we could go home in time for me to go swimming.

I bent over, took a match out of my pocket, scraped it swiftly across a rock on the ground, and watched as the head of the match burst into a tiny bright flame. Then I tossed it into the patch of sagebrush. The *whoosh* and *crackle* of the blaze began immediately, and it headed in a straight line toward the gate and Aunt Laurie and me. This was not what I had planned at all. I stood frozen for the second time that day, even though the heat was close to me now. Aunt Laurie straightened up and turned around, and a look of shock and horror swept across her face.

"Oh, my Lord, fire!" she screamed. "Get out of here, quick!"

I don't remember moving, but suddenly she had me by the hand, pulling me ahead of the line of fire. We ran with the little flames licking at our heels. As Aunt Laurie struggled to open the gate, I noticed that she no longer had her bucket. She had thrown it down somewhere along the way. I was moving under my own power now, and I hurried through the gate and held it open for her. She was holding up her long skirt so it would not catch fire, but she made it through the gate ahead of the flames.

I could hear other voices yelling now, and I saw Mr. Othie and some neighbor men had come to fight the fire and keep it from spreading to Mr. Othie's barn and house and the neighbors' fields, too.

Aunt Laurie headed straight down the road toward my house, with me lagging behind. I knew what I was in for as soon as she told Mom what had happened and I had no desire to hurry. By the time I got home, Mom was fully informed and ready with the switch in her hand.

"Get in here, little Meanness," she yelled at me. "What on earth did you think you were doing?"

Aunt Laurie went on home to recover and left me to Mom and the switch. When Mom had finished nettling my legs, she sent me inside to wait until Dad came home.

"You'll get another whipping from him," Mom assured me. "We're not raising a little fire bug. Nobody will want to see you coming!"

Facing Dad was what I dreaded more than anything. It was his talks that hurt the most when he was disappointed in me. He was disappointed that night and, instead of spanking me, he sat me down to point out what I had done wrong.

"You could have burned Mr. Othie's barn and house," he pointed out. "It could have reached the neighbors."

It took a long time to live that one down. The neighbors, and even Jerry, laughed at me when they heard what I had done. They knew it was just a boyish prank, done with no thought for the consequences; but they made life hard with their teasing for a while.

I never set another fire. And I'm sure it was just a coincidence that Jerry grew up to be a firefighter and arson investigator!

Explosive Idea

Even though I learned my lesson about matches when I burned the sage field, I still had a thing or two to learn about fireworks.

When I was a boy, fireworks were legal in Kentucky, so firecrackers were easy to come by. What I really liked were cherry bombs. They were loud and powerful and shook everything around them when they were set off.

I still had several left over from the Fourth of July when school was well underway one fall. It was cold enough to have a fire in the big pot-bellied stove in our one-room school, and Mr. Grady, the teacher, appointed two different boys each day to be in charge of building the fire each morning.

The day came when my friend Ed and I were selected to be the fire-starters. It was a day when I really did not want to be at school. My dad and a couple of his friends had planned to go hunting and I wanted to go with them.

"You have to go to school, son," Dad told me. "Maybe we can go hunting over the weekend."

I didn't want to wait until the weekend. I wanted to go today. The sun was shining, and there was just enough nip in the air to lure any self-respecting boy from a stuffy schoolroom. The thought occurred to me that, even though I might have to go to school, I didn't have to stay. I felt the cherry bombs in my pocket and I got an idea. Maybe I could do something to make Mr. Grady send us all home. I thought a mild explosion in the stove might make him think something was wrong and that he would send us home until he could check it out.

Mr. Grady rang the bell and the students took their seats. Ed and I went to the stove to start the fire, while Mr. Grady had the students begin their work. We soon had the fire going and I pulled the cherry bombs from my pocket and revealed them to Ed. I pointed toward the stove. Ed's eyes got big and he shook his head, but he didn't do anything to draw Mr. Grady's attention. He just stepped back as I tossed the cherry bombs into the stove. Then both of us hurried to our seats.

I think our hurry to sit down might have made Mr. Grady suspicious. He turned around and looked at us just as the cherry bombs exploded—BOOM! BOOM! BOOM!

He might have thought it was just something in the wood, except the explosion was so loud it shook the stove and blew the stove door open. Sparks and burning coals flew all over the floor near the stove, and students jumped and ran screaming from their seats.

I don't remember a lot about what happened next. Everything else was a big blur as my good sense took over and focused on one thing. *I knew I was in big trouble!*

Mr. Grady beat out the flames and settled the students back in their seats. Then he beat my bottom and settled me in the corner facing the wall. He started to do the same to Ed, but I saved him by confessing that I was the one who'd done it. Ed still wasn't off the hook, though, because he knew and didn't tell what I was going to do. Mr. Grady kept us both in at recess and made us work while everybody else got to go outside and enjoy the perfect autumn day.

The worse part was after school when Mr. Grady drove me home to tell my parents.

"What on earth made you do such a thing?" Dad wanted to know. "You could have burned the school down."

I had no defense. I had been caught red-handed.

The worst thing was that I didn't get to go hunting on Saturday. Dad took me out to the woods and made me cut enough wood to last the school for a month.

And, of course it goes without saying, I was not allowed to have cherry bombs again for a long, long time!

Sunday Pastimes
(Or Adventures With Cat Scratcher)

When I was a boy growing up in the country, there weren't any computer games and I-Pods to entertain us. We had to create our own diversions. I went to school and helped my dad work on weekdays and Saturdays, so Sunday after church was the only time that was truly my own.

Most men and boys did not look forward to church on Sunday morning, unless there was a special young lady to see, but it was the main social gather for the community. For most of us, church meant sitting through boring sermons, sweating in the summer and freezing in the winter, while the preacher droned on or screamed at us to change our ways or go to Hell. Most of the men came with their wives and children, but remained outside to visit, trade knives and watches, or take a swig of whiskey from a jug they kept hidden in the spring below the church. Until we boys reached a suitable age to join them, we were hauled inside, seated on a hard pew, and expected to remain awake and well behaved through the off-key singing and long-winded sermons. We considered it a gift directly from God when any occurrence gave us some comic relief from our boredom.

We boys had one neighborhood hero that we could count on to liven things up during a dull Sunday service. He was a young man in his early twenties who went by the name of Cat Scratcher because he would fight anything and often have scratches to show for it.

His first memorable escapade happened one Sunday morning in early summer. The church was getting an addition for Sunday school rooms and lumber was stacked by the side of the building to be used in the construction. There was no air-conditioning, so the doors and windows were left open for air to circulate for the congregation. The service had begun and all was going well inside the small house of worship.

Outside, things were not going so well for a local rabbit. He came hopping into the churchyard just as my hound dog that had followed me to church and had picked a shady spot to wait for me, raised up to stretch and look around. The dog spotted the rabbit and the rabbit spotted the dog. The dog began to bay and the rabbit bolted to a hiding place under the lumber with my hound in hot pursuit. The rabbit reached safety, but the hound continued to bay, trying unsuccessfully to get to the rabbit. Cat Scratcher decided to lend a hand to the hound. He managed to grab the rabbit and pull him from his hiding place. He held him in the air while the hound leapt and barked furiously.

Maybe Cat Scratcher was a fan of *Tom Sawyer's* or maybe he was just naturally creative, but the opportunity was too perfect to pass up. He moved quickly to the church door and set the rabbit free in the aisle. Down ran the rabbit and down ran the dog! They rounded the pulpit and streaked down the aisle again. As the rabbit made his exit, someone kicked the hound and brought the race to an end. It started a fight, though, as Cat Scratcher defended my hound. Cat Scratcher was hauled off to jail and, when the service ended, my hound and I were hauled off home where we got a good scolding. I thought it was worth it. I hope Cat Scratcher did, too.

To me, Cat Scratcher's master prank came on a hot summer day when I thought I was going to melt in my seat before the sermon ended. Fanning only moved the hot air around, but brought no relief. Cat Scratcher and some of the men emptied the whisky bottle down at the spring below the church and, when Cat Scratcher started to throw the bottle away, he spied a nest of yellow jackets at the side of a stump. He was inspired by what we boys thought was a daring idea. He put the bottle by the nest and tapped the stump gently. The yellow jackets immediately swarmed into the bottle and Cat Scratcher popped on the lid.

It was common knowledge that there was a knothole under the pulpit. Any boy or young man worth his salt filed away bits of information like that in case they could ever be used. Cat Scratcher remembered that knothole and knew it was crucial to his plan. The church sat off the ground on blocks, so Cat Scratcher had plenty of room to crawl underneath. He reached the knothole, opened the bottle and let the yellow jackets loose to do their thing.

The preacher was at a very important point in his sermon.

"Repent!" he shouted. "Repent or you will go to Hell...HELL..AHHHHH!"

In total amazement, we watched the preacher dance around the pulpit, pulling at his clothes! It soon became evident that this was not a holy dance, because the yellow jackets came after the people in the front row, and then the next, and the next. People raced for the door and tumbled out the windows. Some swatted, some were stung, and some, like me who knew it was not a bad thing to sit near the back in spite of what everybody else did, were lucky enough to escape.

Escape was not in the cards for Cat Scratcher., though. Some of the more righteous men saw him crawling out and detained him until the sheriff came and took him away. Service ended for the day, but I stopped long enough to thank the Lord for the happiest feeling I ever had in that church!

Down ran the rabbit and down ran the dog! They rounded
the pulpit and streaked down the aisle again.

Lonnie E. Brown

The "Opossum Walker"

After church on Sunday, we would have Sunday dinner and then we were free to indulge in our own pursuits. Often neighbors would drop by or relatives would come to visit. On hot days, the older folks would move to a shady spot on the front porch or under a tree, while the children read, played games, or went fishing.

My favorite pastime on Sunday afternoons was to slip away from the others and roam through the fields and woods and see what I could find. My favorite place to relax and think by myself was the wooded area down the road behind our house. I observed all kinds of interesting things in nature in different seasons.

One Sunday, some neighbors dropped by to visit, and Mom sent Dad to the country store down the road to get some things she needed to cook supper. Since the owner lived beside the store, he opened it anytime someone came to buy something. I saw this as a good time to go for a walk. I thought I might find where some quails were nesting.

I came upon a thicket by a little branch when I heard a rustling noise. I stopped and listened. The rustling sounded again, and I stood there expecting to see a rabbit emerge. To my surprise, the matted weeds parted and out came a big opossum!

It wasn't unusual for the possum to be near the little branch because they often make their dens there, but it was unusual to see the opossum in the afternoon. Opossums are nocturnal, spending most of the day in their dens and coming out at night to look for food. Opossums eat just about anything—roots, snails, insects, fruit, vegetables, etc.—and this one looked like he had found plenty to satisfy his diet.

Of course, what the opossum may not have been aware of was that opossums were a very satisfying part of human diets in the country. He didn't seem to regard me as an enemy, though. The opossum's first defense when it feels threatened is to "sull up" or "play dead." We sometimes call acts like this *playing opossum.* The animal's brain and nervous system reacts to fear by automatically sending the opossum into a catatonic state, which lowers the heartbeat and respiration. If cornered, it also responds by growling, hissing, and baring its 50 sharp teeth. This opossum's system must have been out of whack, because it did none of these things. It just looked at me and went about its business of sniffing and checking out things.

I was intrigued by this behavior. I picked up a long, sturdy stick and gently nudged the possum, thinking it would hiss or sull. It did neither. It just moved in the direction I indicated. That gave me an idea. Since we had company, I thought Mom might like to have a big, fat opossum for supper. Since it was being so cooperative, I figured I'd just walk Mr. Opossum home for supper. I nudged him again and off we went. Now and then he would stop to check something out with a sniff, and then he was once again on course.

We came out of the woods, crossed the field, and headed down the main road. Cars began to stop while people stuck their heads out the window to look. A boy walking down the road with a 'possum trotting along beside him was not an ordinary sight. Their expressions of amazement fell on deaf ears as far as the opossum was concerned, and we continued on to my house.

Our neighbor, Moreland, saw us coming first.

"Look at that!" he said. "What will that boy do next?"

Mom wasn't as enthusiastic as I thought she'd be.

"There must be something wrong with it if it's not sulling. I'm not cooking that thing!"

Dad returned from the store about that time, and he was more impressed. Mom stood firm, however.

I put the opossum under a washtub, with a side propped up with a small rock to give the opossum some air. I brought it food and water for about three days, hoping my mom would change her mind about cooking my catch. The opossum ate and drank and seemed perfectly content, but Mom insisted that I should let it go. She outlasted me, and I finally raised the tub and gave the opossum his freedom.

He seemed a little confused at first, so I nudged him in the right direction and he took off back to the thicket by the branch. My first attempt to bring home food for the table ended. I did not become known as a great hunter. People just called me the "Possum Walker."

Nature Study

Sometimes on lazy afternoons, I conducted nature studies that I did not tell my mom about. If my pursuits involved a close encounter with an animal or insect, I could count on a lecture about the possibility of getting hurt, or a scolding about being *an aggravating little thing* that should behave myself and not bother little innocent creatures. That's why I learned what I could and filed it away in my head in case I ever had a use for it. Sometimes my mischief resulted in actually learning some lessons that I could apply to my life later.

One such experience was my encounter with a mud dauber wasp. Mud daubers are solitary wasps that construct small nests of mud in or around sheds, barns, or under open structures or similar sites. Mud daubers should be regarded as beneficial. They rarely sting and they catch disagreeable spiders or insects, which they sting and paralyze and place in their nests in a series of cells. They lay a single egg on the prey, and seal the cell with mud. Then the female departs and does not return. The larvae that hatch from the eggs feed on the prey until it's time to emerge and start the process all over. Mud nests can easily be scraped off and discarded when they are no longer used.

I was on one of my afternoon walks that had not turned up anything of interest. I was almost home when I noticed the mud dauber fly under a storage shed that Dad had built near the house. I had nothing more interesting to do, so I crawled under the shed to see where it was going. I saw that it was in the process of constructing a nest.

I knew that females collected mud, rolled it into a ball, carried it to the nest, and molded it into place with its mandibles. This one had the nest well under way and was adding ringed layers of mud at this point. It ignored me and flew away for another mud ball.

I very carefully reached up and removed the mud ring it had just attached to the nest. Then I waited. In a few minutes, the dauber returned with another mud ball. It seemed puzzled, but it went to work. I watched without moving or making a sound as it applied another round of mud and flew off again. Again, I reached up and carefully removed the last mud layer. I got back in my hiding place and waited again. Shortly, the dauber returned with another load. It was really frustrated now. It couldn't figure out what was wrong, but it knew it was not making any progress. It checked out the entire nest, going up and over and all around. It finally added the last load and few off again. Again, I moved in fast and took off the newly applied mud. I was really curious now about what it would do when it came back. I didn't have to wait long. The poor dauber returned, saw that the mud was gone again, and made a wise decision. She dropped the ball of mud and flew away. Although I waited a long time, she never came back.

I crawled out from under the shed and went on home. I didn't tell anybody what I did that day, but I learned a valuable lesson that day from a little wasp: When you see you aren't getting anywhere despite your best efforts, just cut your losses, and move on!

Influenced

I wouldn't want to hold anybody but myself responsible for my misdeeds, but I think now that taking the mud off the mud dauber's nest could have been influenced by a story of a neighborhood prank that one of our neighbors pulled on another one night. I always enjoyed it, even though I wouldn't have enjoyed it if the prank had been played on me.

Playing practical jokes was a favorite pastime in those days because there was very little entertainment offered in our community. We had to provide our own fun, and, sometimes, young men didn't realize that their pranks were unkind. This tale belongs in that category.

Old Jim lived in a one-room cabin in our neighborhood, right down the road from a teenage boy named Ray. Despite the age difference, the two liked each other, but that didn't stop Ray from playing a joke on Old Jim whenever the opportunity arose. Old Jim's mind was a bit slow, so this made him a good target for teenagers like Ray who were looking for good-natured fun and were unaware that they were sometimes out of line.

One night Old Jim worked in the fields until dark. He stopped by the barn to feed and milk his cows, and Ray just happened to be going home and saw him. Those were the good days when people could leave their doors unlocked without worrying about being robbed. Old Jim never worried about intruders, but, on this night, he should have. Ray thought it would be funny to sneak inside and hide under the bed and scare Old Jim when he came inside. Ray didn't have long to wait until Old Jim came in, put the milk away, and noticed the wood box was empty. He immediately went outside and carried in some wood and placed it by the stove in the box.

To understand the success of the prank, one should know the layout of the cabin. The bed under which Ray was hiding was right by the stove and the wood box. Old Jim opened the stove door and put in a stick of wood in preparation to cook some supper. He went back out to get more wood, and Ray reached out and removed the wood from the stove, placing it quickly back in the box.

Ray could see Old Jim return with another load of wood from his position under the bed. He saw him scratch his head and squint his face in a puzzled look. He reached over, picked up the stick of wood, and again placed it in the stove. When he went out for a third load, Ray struck again, repeating the process. A sharper man might have caught on to the prank sooner, but poor Jim was a little dull.

When Old Jim came in this time, he looked down at the box, shook his head as if to clear it, and looked around the room. Then he put the wood in the stove again and reached for the matches.

At this point, Ray's luck ran out. Old Jim must have seen a movement from the corner of his eye, because he turned around just as Ray's arm shot out from under the bed. Old Jim yelled something Ray couldn't understand or didn't care to repeat, and he grabbed another stick of wood and began to beat Ray's arm. Ray was yelling, too, and by the time he made Old Jim understand who he was and that he was just playing a joke, he had several cuts and bruises and a few splinters to remove.

Old Jim cooled down and never held a grudge. He still didn't lock his door, but he was sharp enough to look under his bed at night, and Ray was sharp enough never to be under there again.

Under Cover of Darkness

Nighttime was the best time for playing practical jokes. When young men in their teens or very early twenties worked hard in the fields all day, they were ready to ramble and rustle up some fun as soon as the sun went down.

Tom (who would become my father-in-law) and his best friend Edgar set out one dark summer night to play a trick on a farmer who lived nearby. It wasn't the first time they had paid this man a visit or indulged in the same routine. It was simple enough, but the farmer never seemed to catch on. Tom and Edgar would take a couple of cowbells, hide in the farmer's cornfield and began ringing the bells. The farmer, thinking the cows were in the corn, would light his lantern and come running out to round them up. As soon as he would come out, Tom and Edgar would be quiet and the farmer would think he was mistaken. As soon as he'd go back inside, Tom and Edgar would move to a different part of the field and ring the bells again. When the farmer had come out several times, looking tired and mystified, the two pranksters would get bored and go home.

On this dark summer night, fate stepped in to make it a night of reckoning for the two young men. Thunder rumbled in the distance and lightning streaked across the sky as they approached the farmhouse. Neither worried about storms. Besides, they thought they would have time to bring the farmer out for a few searches before the storm actually broke. They were very, very wrong.

They had not brought lanterns, but they had come equipped with the cowbells and the gun that Tom always carried. Before they could ring the bells, clouds swirled overhead and rain poured from the sky. At the same time, a huge ball of light hovered over the farmhouse and rained down like fire while the stunned boys watched. They ran for shelter in a shed by the side of the yard, and they could see though the window that the farmer's wife was ill in bed, tended by some neighbor women. They took the fireball as a warning that they might truly upset her with their antics, so they waited until the rain settled into a lighter beat, and they headed home.

Their retreat was uneventful until they came to the banks of the little creek they had to cross to get home. The water was high from the rain and it flowed swiftly under the foot log they had to walk on. One wrong step in the dark on that narrow foot log, and they would fall into the flooded creek and be swept away. Then they felt that some higher power decided to reward them for not bothering the farmer and his wife that night. A little light, like foxfire, appeared at the end of the foot log and guided them safely across. When they reached the other side of the swollen creek, the little light disappeared as mysteriously as it had come.

The boys walked in silence until they came to Edgar's house.

"You can come in and spend the night," Edgar offered.

Tom declined. They would be expecting him home and he didn't want his mother to worry. He only had to cross a couple of fields and he would be there. He said goodnight and went on his way. He no longer had his best friend with him, but he had his gun. He felt safe enough.

Tom had gone about half way through the field when a flash of lightning showed a dark form in the fencerow up ahead. The lightning wasn't too bright now, but Tom thought the thing moved when he did. He stopped and the thing in the fencerow stopped, too. It was waiting right by the path he had to take. He pulled out his gun and felt great comfort in the familiar feel of it.

"Who's there?" he called, taking a step forward.

There was no answer, but it seemed to move closer.

"Speak or I'll shoot!" he called.

There was no answer. They just moved closer together. Tom aimed at the target. He was a good shot. He didn't have to worry.

Tom fired and saw the thing move. He had hit it, but it still kept coming. With his nerves already on edge, Tom fired four more times, and each time, he could tell he had hit it. Still it stood upright.

Tom had one bullet left and he had to make good with it.

I won't fire until I am face to face with the thing, he thought.

It was dark, but he knew he was too close to miss. He fired his last shot and rushed up to see what enemy waited there in the darkness. He couldn't believe it. He had shot the top out of a little bush.

He told that story often. He said it taught him about Divine Intervention and humility. And it taught him never to fire a gun unless he knew what he was shooting at!

Courtin' Tricks

The young men who didn't have girls to court were always making life difficult for those who did--especially if the young suitor was bashful or uneasy about being out alone at night.

Many dates were like group dates. Boys walked girls home from school or church. Schools and churches sometimes had cakewalks or pie suppers that were very successful social events, as well as good fundraisers. Girls would bake cakes or make pies and put them in beautiful boxes decorated with crepe paper and bows. Boys bid on the boxes and the winner got to eat with the girl! Nobody was supposed to know which box belonged to what girl, but if a couple had a special interest in each other, they managed to get the information to the right party.

Sometimes, a boy would just go to a girl's home and court her there with the family all around. Some homes had a courting candle that could be set to burn at different levels. If the family wanted the young man to leave early, they set the candle to burn down quickly. They set it for a slower burn if they approved. Sometimes, the father would simply announce bedtime. Then the young man left without protest.

There was one young lady who had the admiration and attention of two young men in the neighborhood. One was something of a bully who didn't take it too kindly when she chose a polite young fellow considered to be something a wimp. The rejected bully decided to give him a little scare. He enlisted one of his friends to help him.

They knew that he went to call on the young lady every Saturday night and that he always took the same road home. They knew what time he left the young lady's house to head home. Since it was Saturday night, the young lady's father usually permitted the young man to stay until about eleven-thirty. That put him on the road home a little before midnight.

They had hidden and watched him a couple of times, and noticed him looking over his shoulder and whistling nervously as he hurried along in the dark. He jumped at the slightest noise, and they saw that he was especially uneasy walking past the graveyard that was right beside the road. Unfortunately for him, there was no alternate route for him to take. They observed that he reached this spot just about midnight, and he would almost break into a run to get by as fast as he could.

Perfect, they thought. The witching hour!

Fate seemed to be working with them. Everybody loved to tell stories about ghostly sightings in that graveyard, so they were sure the young man had heard plenty of the old tales. It would make a perfect background for their prank.

They picked a night with a full moon to put their plan in action. The moonlight gave the eerie shadows a life of their own. They knew the effect it would have on their intended victim. They stopped to laugh at the very thought of it as they made their preparations. If they could scare him off, maybe the bully would have a chance to be in her good graces.

They fixed up a straw dummy and dressed him in pants, a shirt, coat, and a hat. They were proud of their handiwork, because he looked quite real when they stepped out into the road and looked at him from that distance. They tied a rope around his waist and propped him up against an old oak tree that stood right at the corner of the graveyard. They ran the rope over a limb, climbed up the tree, and sat holding the rope, waiting for the nervous young man to come along.

The two watched the young man come into sight. He was hurrying along at a pretty good gait as he approached the graveyard. He looked over his shoulders and whistled softly, either to comfort himself by a human sound or to scare the boogers away.

The two pranksters knew the instant he spotted the dummy. He stopped dead in his tracks. He could see what he thought was a man leaning against the tree in the moonlight, and for a few seconds, he was undecided about his course of action. Then, being the polite young man he was, he spoke.

"Good evening, Sir!"

There was no answer. The two in the tree pulled the rope just enough to make the dummy come off the ground and return to its original position.

The young man wasn't certain of what he just saw. The man had moved, but it was an unnatural movement. Maybe his eyes were playing tricks on him. He had heard strange tales about this place, but he didn't really believe he could be standing there looking at a ghost!

"Good evening, Sir," the young man repeated, coming closer. There was a crack in his voice when he spoke this time.

Suddenly, the bully and his friend groaned and gave the rope a yank. Before the young man's startled eyes, the straw man shot straight up the tree trunk. No natural man would do that!

The young man's mouth flew open. He swayed back and forth for a few seconds, staring in disbelief.

"AHH! AHH!" he screamed.

Clutching his chest, he shot off down the road

"AHH! AHH!" he kept screaming.

The bully and his friend jumped from the tree and rolled on the ground, laughing as they heard his cries farther and farther in the distance.

Then something else caught their attention. They heard another sound!

"Shh," said the bully, nudging his friend. "What is that?"

They both listened. Something was moving among the tombstones. For an instant, their hearts nearly stopped. *Could the stories be true? Was the old cemetery really haunted?* Neither was too eager to stay around and investigate.

"Let's get out of here," whispered the friend.

Without another word, both started backing slowly into the road, ready to take flight as they watched something white emerge from the shadows.

That did it! Both were off and running for home as if their feet had wings. They could hear the thing grunting behind them, but they could tell it was losing ground. The grunts were getting fainter.

Breathless and with pains stabbing their sides, they slowed down and risked a look back.

With great relief, they both sank to the ground laughing as they realized it was just Silas Burton's old hog that had gotten out of its pen on the adjoining farm. The two got up, went home, and felt quite satisfied with the night's event.

The nervous young man had not fared so well, though. He had been frightened beyond reason. The poor fellow ran every step of the way home. They said he didn't open the door when he got there. He broke it down as he ran through it and collapsed on the other side.

He was so frightened that he nearly had a heart attack. His folks had to take him to the doctor. He never fully recovered and would never go out alone again at night.

The bully succeeded in breaking up the budding romance, but it didn't do him any good. His rival never went back to court the girl, but, when the story came out about the cruel prank, the girl wouldn't have anything to do with the bully.

Who's Chasing Whom?

A good chase or a run for your life was always material for a good laugh in the country. Sometimes someone bolted for his life without even being set up for a scare.

My friend Jerry and I rarely ran from anything. We'd taken President Roosevelt's words to heart and believed that *The only thing we had to fear was fear itself!* We should have reminded a neighborhood buddy, R.G., of this theory one night when we got a hankering for watermelon and decided to raid Mr. Blankenship's watermelon patch.

It had been a hot summer day and, as night fell, our desire rose for a cool, ripe, juicy watermelon. Everybody knew that Mr. Blankenship grew the best ones around. Usually, the old man didn't mind if we neighbor boys sneaked in and took a watermelon or two to enjoy for our own purposes. His attitude had changed recently, though.

Milt Simpson's nephew, Lenzo, had come down from Cincinnati to visit for a couple of weeks, and he didn't know much about the value of growing things. As what he thought was a prank, Lenzo had taken a tobacco stick one night and stabbed about a half a row of watermelons before his Uncle Milt caught him. That was one exception to President Roosevelt's theory. When Milt caught him, Lenzo actually did have more to fear than fear itself.

Even though Milt made Lenzo confess and pay Mr. Blankenship for the watermelons he destroyed, Mr. Blankenship was left feeling riled up and ungenerous when it came to tolerating any more midnight raids. He'd even gone so far as to spread the word that anyone who tried to gain entry to his prized patch could count on leaving with a load of buckshot instead of watermelons. Jerry and I couldn't resist the temptation to try to outwit him.

On this particular hot summer night, Mr. Blankenship's challenge fed our desire to sneak in and steal one of those thirst-quenching melons. Our friend R.G. begged to join us.

"You get scared easy," said Jerry. "Do you think you can be quiet?"

"I'm sure I can," said RG, but he didn't sound too convincing, "Just give me a chance."

Jerry and I looked at each other and finally nodded in agreement.

"Okay," said Jerry. "We'll see you tonight."

We waited until everybody was asleep and then slipped out and met at RG's house. RG had evidently been giving the matter some thought, and now he was hesitant to participate.

"Maybe we shouldn't go," he said. "Mr. Blankenship does have a shotgun!"

"Come on," said Jerry. "You know he's not going to shoot anybody!"

"That's right," I joined in. "He just said that to scare people off. He wouldn't really do it."

We started off across the field and RG reluctantly followed, with my dog, Brownie, bringing up the rear. We walked without speaking. It was a cloudy night, with the moon peeking out only now and then as we entered the edge of the field farthest away from Mr. Blankenship's house. There were no lights showing and no sign of movement, so we felt certain he was sound asleep.

"I don't like this," whispered RG. "What if he's hiding with a gun?"

We ignored him and moved silently between the rows. R.G. trailed at our heels, looking over his shoulder. Jerry and I each pulled a choice watermelon from a vine, and RG started to, when a terrible commotion broke out behind us. At that exact instant, the clouds broke and the moon broke through for just a second. It was just long enough for Jerry and me to see Brownie take off after a rabbit. Just as a precaution, Jerry and I ducked down out of sight in case the noise should arouse Mr. Blankenship.

R.G. whirled around, but by now, the moon was gone and it was so dark he couldn't see us. He heard Brownie and the rabbit running and thought it was Jerry and me. He was in full panic now. He thought Mr. Blankenship must be coming after us to make us run like that. R.G. took off after Brownie and the rabbit, screaming, "Wait for me, boys! Wait for me!"

Jerry and I, still clutching our precious loot, took off after R.G.

"Stop!" we shouted. "Stop!"

This only seemed to make him run faster. We finally realized that he thought it was Mr. Blankenship hollering at him. We just stopped and watched him streak out of sight toward his house. Of course, we could have caught him, but it was hard carrying those two big watermelons. We just sat down laughing in the middle of the field, took out our pocketknives, and opened up the sweetest, juiciest melons we ever ate in our lives. It is true that forbidden fruit really is the best.

Brownie soon returned empty-handed from his fruitless chase and lay down, completely unaware of the havoc he'd created just moments before. I could have sworn I heard a low chuckle off in the distance, but I couldn't be sure. If Mr. Blankenship saw what happened, he never mentioned it. I'm sure that if he did see the show we put on that night, he would have thought it was well worth the price of two watermelons.

Freda and The Little Hairy Man

"AHH! AHH! AHH!"

The screams coming up Russell Creek Hollow startled the workers in the tobacco patch so much that they stopped chopping weeds and leaned on their hoes.

"AHH! AHH! AHH!"

They watched as young Freda Nolin burst from the woods, pale and gasping for breath as she held her sides.

"What's the matter?" Bill Nolin called to his daughter.

"Little hairy man," she answered, still trying to catch her breath.

"What on earth are you talking about?" Bill asked.

"A little hairy man came in the house," she said, still breathing hard. "I spoke, but he wouldn't answer me! He screeched and ran up and down the door."

Laughter ripped through the tobacco patch.

"He did what?" Bill asked, moving closer to his daughter.

"He grabbed a banana off the table," she continued, "and then he ran out the door and up a tree! He just sat on a limb chattering at me!"

Laughter roared through the tobacco patch at that, and Bill Nolin even smiled. He put his arm around his daughter and gave her a drink of water.

"Sit down over here in the grass," he told her. "I think I can explain what happened."

Freda Nolin had just had her first meeting with a monkey—something she had never seen before—and to her, the encounter had not been funny!

Lonnie E. Brown

Freda learned that day that Will Harrington, who owned the general store a couple of miles down the road, had purchased a monkey from a traveling circus several weeks before. He had tied it out front, thinking it would attract business. Freda had not been to the circus or the store, so she knew nothing about it. She had not been with her father and his friends when they were talking about the monkey, either, so she had no knowledge at all of Mr. Harrington's new attraction. She had no TV or newspaper, so she'd never even seen a picture of a monkey.

On the day that Freda and the monkey were destined to meet, she had stayed home to cook dinner for the work hands. It was a warm day, so Freda left the doors open for the air to circulate through the house. Most houses back then had no screens doors or windows to keep out animals, birds, or insects out.

Freda was well along with her preparations for the midday meal, unaware that the stage was being set for one of the most dramatic events of her life.

Down the road at Harrington's General Store, the tied-up money got bored with his restricted space and decided it would be more interesting to be free. He deftly untied the rope that held him and took off exploring new territory. He simply followed the creek, swinging from tree to tree until he arrived at the Nolin house.

Inside, Freda had just removed the cornbread from the oven and set it on the table by a bowl of fresh fruit. The smell of the fresh-baked bread, or more likely the bananas in the bowl, drifted through the air and caught the monkey's attention. He evidently thought this was a good place to stop and eat.

THUMP!

The monkey landed on the floor by the door, where it remained checking out Freda.

Freda jumped at the sudden noise and whirled around to see what had caused it. She could hardly believe her eyes. There stood a little man completely covered by hair.

She was totally at a loss for words.

"CHEEEEE!" screeched the monkey.

Freda was dumbfounded. Most likely, anybody would have reacted the same way if they'd never seen a monkey before, and, like Freda, anybody could have mistaken the strange, short creature for a little hairy man.

Freda finally managed to speak.

"How-howdy, Mister," she said. "What do you want?"

"CHEE-CHEE-CHEEEE!" it screeched with a big money grin, and it waddled toward the table.

Freda had never seen such big teeth or such an ugly mouth in her life. The poor girl was scared half to death. She backed around the table as the little hairy visitor leapt on the table top with a single bound. He snatched a banana and chattered happily as he peeled it and began to eat.

By now Freda had backed into a corner where she had propped the broom after she swept earlier. She grabbed the broom and came out swinging.

"Git!" she shouted. "Git out of here! Git!"

The money jumped off the table, raced out the door and up a tree, where he sat happily on a limb eating his lunch.

Freda saw her chance and lost no time making her escape. She ran up the hollow screaming until she reached the tobacco patch.

It seemed like a good time to take a break, so Bill Nolin, his work hands, and Freda returned down the hollow to the house.

Mr. Harrington had missed his monkey and arrived searching for it at the same time that the group got to the house. He was able to coax it down with another banana and took it back to the store again.

Mr. Harrington built a big escape-proof cage for the monkey and put a swing and bars inside. Customers sat on the porch and watched the monkey's antics for a long time to come. Even though they enjoyed it, Freda never felt very enthusiastic about it. She hardly ever came to the store at all.

Folks said she would never even date a man with a beard, and I know for a fact the man she finally married was definitely clean-shaven!

Boogers and Other Things

If we'd admit it, we've all had our share of embarrassing moments with animals. I know I have. One that I had to live down in my family started at dusk one night when my dad told me to go to the store and get some oil for our lamps.

We had been trying for some time to get electricity in the homes on our road, but so far we were unsuccessful. Ours was one of eight families that had to agree to the service before the electricity company would put up the poles and do the wiring. Four of us wanted electricity. The other four were holding off because they were afraid that wiring their houses might cause their houses to catch fire. Electricity was a new thing, and some people didn't know enough about it to take a chance.

Dad and I came home late on this afternoon from our milk route. Mom met us at the door with the news that we were out of oil. We'd need some for the lamps that night and for starting a fire for breakfast the next morning. Dad needed to check the right front tire on our truck, so I was elected to go make the purchase.

I was tired from lifting and loading and unloading milk cans, and all I wanted to do was eat supper and rest. I never understood why this lack of oil couldn't be taken care of during the daytime. Of course, Mr. Harrington opened his store at any hour when a neighbor needed something because he lived next door to his store, so nobody had to confine their purchases to the daylight hours.

I didn't like to admit it, but I didn't like to go to Mr. Harrington's store after dark. The road led through a strip of woods where men used to gather by a little bridge and gamble. There was a story that supposedly was true about a man being killed in those woods over a gambling debt. Some people swore his spirit walked the woods at night, looking to get his money back! I didn't really believe in ghosts, but the woods were full of strange sounds and shadows that often made me shiver and quicken my steps, especially as I neared the bridge.

"Hurry up," Mom called to me. "I need to fill up the lamps."

I picked up the oilcan and started off down the road. I whistled for my dog Brownie to join me and keep the boogers away, but nobody knew that reason but me. Just as we got to the edge of the woods, Brownie spied a rabbit and took off in the opposite direction. I knew I was on my own.

I hurried through the woods and arrived at Mr. Harrington's store just as the last rays of sun vanished in the west. I made my purchase quickly, discouraging any small talk from Mr. Harrington, and headed with my oilcan down the road and into the woods. It was then that I realized I hadn't brought a light with me. I'd been down the road many times and I knew every stone and hole, but I now felt completely enveloped in inky darkness

I walked carefully so I wouldn't spill the oil, and I was covering the distance pretty well when I heard it. Something was walking along the road behind me! The sound was soft, but steady. I hurried, but it came right along, keeping a consistent distance between the two of us.

I wanted to turn around to see if I could tell what it was, but I knew it was too dark to see. I was too scared to call out, so I just walked a little faster. The steps behind me came faster, too. Goosebumps were rising all over my body. I was nearing the bridge and the footsteps were now getting closer.

Could there be such a thing as ghosts? Could that dead man really be walking behind me in the dark?

By now, my imagination was in full swing. I thought of men gambling and becoming angry. I pictured them killing the poor man over money. I knew he was behind me now. He was coming closer and closer, and I was becoming more frightened by the minute.

Then suddenly, something like two hands touched my back. I whirled around, flinging my arms and letting the can of oil fly out of my hand and into the weeds by the side of the road. I stood trembling, sure that I was now in the clutches of a dead man. I leaned over to see what had caught me, and I felt a wet slurp across my face. Slowly my normal senses kicked in and I realized it was Brownie. Evidently, he had tired of chasing the rabbit, picked up my scent, and followed me after all.

In spite of the fact that he had caused me to lose the oil can, I was extremely happy to see

Brownie. I knew that no boogers or ghosts would dare get me with him around.

My heartbeat slowed down and I began to look for the oil can. I found it quickly, but not before most of the oil ran out. I knew I was in trouble then. I didn't have enough money to go back to the store and get more oil.

Brownie and I went on home, and I tried to think of a reason why the can was almost empty. I couldn't say I fell because there was nothing on my clothes to back that up. For lack of a better story, I blamed it on Brownie. I said he jumped up on me and knocked the can out of my hand. I think my pale face and hands that were still a bit shaky gave me away. I could tell that nobody believed me, so I finally told the truth.

All my brothers and sisters laughed at me, of course. Brownie stood around wagging his tail, evidently thinking he had done something great.

Dad just shook his head, got in the truck, and drove to Mr. Harrington's store and bought more oil. I stayed home and listened to Mom's lecture about being a wasteful child when money was so scarce.

There are some things worse than being with spooks in the woods at night. I was in a family that laughed for years because I didn't know the difference in a dog and a dead man walking.

The episode did spare me from anymore nightly excursions for a while. Most of the time until all the neighbors finally agreed to put in electricity, Dad just stopped at the store on the way home and bought us some oil!

Something's In the Chimney

I am still trying to live down one of my encounters with animals, though I still stand by my solution to the problem.

My wife and I moved into a house with a fireplace that hadn't been used for some time. We didn't plan to use the fireplace right away, so we had not had the chimney cleaned out.

I went to bed early one night so I would be fresh for work the next day, and I was just drifting off to sleep when I heard my wife come into the room.

"Honey, get up," she said. "There's something in the chimney."

I opened my eyes slowly and tried to clear my head.

"What?" I asked, not quite sure of what I had heard.

She repeated, "Honey, get up. There is something in the chimney."

I was propped up on my elbow now, trying to digest this news.

"What do you mean?" I asked. "How do you know?"

"I heard something in there," she explained. "I've got the screen across, but I'm afraid it will get out into the house."

"What did it sound like?" I asked, still reluctant to get out of my good warm bed to investigate.

"It was kind of a cross between a growl and a hiss," she said. "I've never heard anything like it."

My wife writes scary stories, so she's always hearing strange things.

"It's just your imagination," I assured her. "Go back to your writing. I'm going back to sleep."

"Get up!" she insisted. "I don't want something getting into the house while we're asleep tonight."

At that point, I decided that sleep at our house that night would be very unlikely that night unless I checked out the chimney. I got up, put on my robe, and followed her to the fireplace.

I listened, but I heard nothing at first. I shined a flashlight up the chimney, but I couldn't see anything.

"I think it's coming from that little ledge in the chimney just out of sight," she said.

"There's nothing there," I assured her. "I'm going back to bed."

Just as I turned to go, I heard it. She was right. It was sort of a cross between a hiss and a growl, but I had heard that sound before. There was no mistaking it. It was a raccoon! I knew at once that a mother racoon had taken up residence in our chimney with her babies!

"It's a mother raccoon with her babies," I informed my wife. "She won't hurt you."

"No, but she could damage the house if she comes inside," my wife replied. "We've got to get her out!"

I didn't see any way of doing that at that time, so I secured the screen so she would be confined to the chimney. Finally, I got back to bed.

The next morning at breakfast, I realized my wife was not going to let things go on as they were.

"As much as I love animals," she said, "she can't live in the chimney. We've got to get her and the babies out without hurting them."

We made a few calls, but we got very little help. We got all sorts of suggestions from just waiting, to building a fire in the fireplace to using mothballs. Just waiting would not make us happy, and building a fire might hurt her and the babies. We didn't want either. Besides, we didn't feel it was safe to light a fire until the chimney had been cleaned. The mothballs were a possibility!

We went to a local department store and bought a supply of mothballs that would have lasted most households a lifetime. The lady at the checkout counter said nothing, but she gave us very strange looks. We rushed home, hoping we had found the solution to our problem.

We tied up the mothballs in a big rag and inserted them in the chimney behind the screen, securing it again so the raccoons would not exit through our house. We wouldn't have had to worry. They did not exit at all. In fact, the mothballs were so stinky that my wife and I almost had to exit the premises. The mother continued to hiss and growl, and we hastily removed the mothballs and threw them away. We were right back at square one.

We sat down in our living room, beaten and discouraged. There had to be a way to evict our unwanted guests, but we didn't know what it could be.

We finally contacted a chimneysweeper who said he thought he could remove the little family without causing any harm, but he couldn't get to us for a couple of days.

Then I had what I still consider was a flash of brilliance.

"What are raccoons afraid of?" I excitedly asked my wife.

"I don't know. What?" she replied.

"Dogs!" I told her, triumphantly.

"But we don't have a dog," she reminded me.

That didn't bother me. I had been around dogs all my life and I could do a great imitation. Without further ado, I got down on the floor on my hands and knees in front of the fireplace and began to bark.

"What are you doing?" my wife cried. "Have you lost your mind?"

Desperate situations call for desperate measures, so I continued to bark. I must have sounded real, because the mother raccoon begin to hiss and growl.

This procedure continued for several minutes.

"ARF! ARF! ARF"

"Hisssss! Growl! Hisss!"

"ARF! ARF! ARF!"

By now, my wife was laughing and searching for the camera. Mercifully, she didn't find it until I discontinued the barking and got to my feet.

The raccoon had decided to cease her response, too, so my wife and I went to bed. The next day and night, we heard nothing. Then, the chimneysweeper finally came. After a careful check, he discovered that the raccoon and her babies were gone!

We had him go ahead and clean the chimney and cap it for a while, just in case the mother decided to return with the little ones. It was a relief to return to a peaceful household.

"See, my barking worked!" I bragged to my wife, quite proud of myself. "I scared her away."

"Humph!" said my wife. "You didn't scare her. As a mother, she just didn't want to raise her babies near a man crazy enough to think he's a dog!"

Snakes, Snakes, Snakes!

When I was growing up, there were some encounters with animals that were not so amusing, unless maybe you were merely a spectator watching what was happening. One of the most frightening things happened on a day when my dad and I expected nothing but fun and relaxation.

It was a warm spring day in the early fifties. Dad and I gathered up our fishing rods and some bait and headed to one of our favorite fishing spots on the Cumberland River above Wolf Creek Dam.

My dad and my future father-in-law helped build Wolf Creek Dam, which was created in 1951 at a cost of $80.4 million. Its main purpose was flood control and the production of hydroelectric power, but it also created the 55,000-acre Lake Cumberland, which would eventually bring a booming tourist business to the area. It probably also created some disturbance in the patterns of wildlife nearby.

On this spring day, the world was quiet, however, and we had the riverbank to ourselves. We baited our hooks, cast our lines out into the water, and sat back waiting for the catfish, bass, and perch to bite. Several accommodated us and we had the beginnings of a fine mess of fish for supper.

The sun rose slowly over the river and we sat admiring the glistening water rippling toward the shore. I saw Dad suddenly lean forward squinting. I looked closely at the water and saw what he was seeing. Neither of us could believe our eyes.

"What the heck is that?" he asked getting to his feet.

I got up, too, but I didn't need to answer him. We could see clearly what was swimming toward us.

"Good Heavens!" I exclaimed.

The river had suddenly turned black. There were snakes, snakes, and more snakes! Neither of us had ever seen anything like it and we never wanted to again. We stood frozen for a minute, staring at the spectacle in front of us in disbelief.

Some of the snakes reached the bank and crawled out of the water. Dad was the first to move as he kicked one away. We struggled to reel in our lines, and finally succeeded.

More snakes were crawling from the river now. Dad grabbed the fish and we held on to our rods.

"Come on, son," Dad ordered. "Let's get out of here right now."

I didn't have to be told twice. We ran for the truck, jumped in, and drove off. We had no idea where the snakes came from, why they came, or where they were going. We just knew we'd never be back at that spot to fish again. And we never were.

People found it hard to believe when Dad and I told that story, but if he were alive today, he'd tell you it was true.

Out Foxed

Once I got myself into a dangerous situation when I went out rambling along the creek by myself. Mom and Dad told me over and over not to go off alone and not tell someone where I was going, but I figured I was smart enough to take care of myself.

One day when Dad was at work and Mom was doing the weekly wash, I took my rifle and set off down the creek toward Buzzard Cave. It was about a mile from the house, and located about thirty feet up on the side of a cliff. I had never seen a buzzard up close and thought I might watch for them to come to the cave and shoot me one.

Mom didn't see me leave, so I didn't bother to tell her where I was going. She wouldn't have allowed me to go if she had known my plan.

I followed the creek bank until I spotted the cave entrance. I sat down to wait for the buzzards to fly in. Nothing happened for about ten minutes. Then I saw something at the cave entrance. It wasn't a buzzard, though. I looked closer and saw two baby red foxes.

This was much better than a buzzard. I had always wanted to catch me a baby fox and raise it for a pet like a dog. This was my chance. I watched, but I saw no sign of the mother fox, so I decided to seize the opportunity to catch a baby fox while she was off hunting.

The cliff was too steep to climb straight up, but the cave was accessible from a narrow ledge that ran around the entire side. I had to go down the creek several yards, wade across, go through the edge of Mr. Conover's pasture, and then climb gradually up until I reached the ledge. I propped my rifle up against a tree in the pasture before I started to climb.

I inched my way up slowly, stepping very carefully along the ledge, which was about two feet wide. I moved quietly so I would not alert the babies. Their keen little noses detected me anyway, and they retreated inside the cave as I neared the entrance.

My back was against the cliff and I looked around, hoping to see a bush or something I could hold onto as I leaned around to look inside. A movement on my left caught my eye. I turned my head to see a very angry mother fox approaching me. She growled once, and that was enough to make me want to be anywhere but on the ledge near her babies. I took a step back, but my foot slipped and I found myself in a nosedive toward the water. I remember hitting extensions from the cliff and landing with such force in the creek that it almost knocked the breath out of me. Fortunately, the water was deep enough to break my fall or I would have broken my neck. I managed to wade to the bank and check the extent of my injuries. I glanced up at the cave, but the mother had gone inside to see about the babies. I saw a bird fly overhead, but, thank goodness, it was not a buzzard. That was the last thing I wanted to see circling me now!

Besides some bruises and some cuts that were bleeding a little, I seem to have survived any major damage in the fall. I walked down to the pasture to retrieve my rifle, but I encountered another obstacle. Mr. Conover's big bull and some of his cows had moved to the shade under the tree and they were eyeing my rifle with some degree of interest. I waited a couple of minutes, but they didn't leave. I finally resorted to throwing some rocks and shouting to scare them away. The cows moved on and the bull, snorting and pawing a couple of times, finally went after them. I dashed in, grabbed my rifle and headed for home.

When I got home, I got scolded by Mom for being out where I shouldn't have been. I wondered if the mother fox scolded her offspring for the very same thing!

Forgotten?

One of my scariest times as a boy was when I was off by myself on one of my first jobs. I didn't wander off that time. Mr. Hadley hired me and drove me way out in the country to work in the woods. He'd already cut some of the big trees, but he hired me to saw up some of the smaller limbs for stove wood. He told me he'd be back to pick me up at four o'clock.

I had my lunch and a jar of water, so I was set for the day. I liked working by myself and I had done this kind of work before with my dad. It was an easy job for me and I was already thinking of how I would spend my money.

Just one thing worried me a little. Mr. Hadley was known to drink at times. Even though my dad knew I was working for him, he didn't know exactly where Mr. Hadley was taking me.

There wasn't a house or barn in sight. It was just the woods and me.

The morning went by quickly. I worked at a steady pace, stopping to drink from my jar of water from time to time. When the sun was straight overhead, I opened my lunch bucket, sat down and leaned against a tree, and ate. Mom had fixed me two fried potato sandwiches with mustard on white bread, and for dessert, she had put in a couple of fried apple pies. I wolfed them down, drank some more water and returned to work.

The day wore on and the sun moved on across the afternoon sky. About mid-afternoon, I heard a low rumble of thunder. I looked west and saw that a dark cloud had moved in. I continued working, hoping the cloud would draw around and go up the river.

BOOM!

The thunder was louder this time and I could tell it was closer. I wasn't normally afraid of storms, but then, normally, I had shelter when a storm actually hit.

CRACK!

A bolt of lightning had come with the thunder that time, and it had struck somewhere. I didn't have a watch, so I didn't know what time it was, but I hoped it was time for Mr. Hadley to come pick me up. I hadn't been watching the sky that closely, but I remembered that it had been fairly low in the sky when I first heard the thunder. Maybe it wouldn't be long. Maybe he would beat the storm.

KER-BOOM!

The thunder was closer than ever. The cloud definitely was not going around. It was headed toward me. My eyes scanned the distance for a sign of Mr. Hadley's truck, but I saw only leaves and grass stirring in the wind. The rain hadn't set in yet, but the doubts did.

What if Mr. Hadley didn't come? What if he had gotten drunk and had forgotten me? Nobody knew where I was but him! How would my dad find me if I didn't get home? Where would I find shelter in the bad storm that was quickly approaching? I wished now that I had saved some of my food and water. I just had a little water left. What if I had to stay here for days?

BOOM! BOOM!

I looked up, but this time the booms weren't thunder. Mr. Hadley's old truck was backfiring as it bumped over the field to pick me up. I think the sight of that old truck was one of the prettiest things I have ever seen.

"Four o'clock!" he said. "Looks like you finished."

"Yeah," I answered, climbing into the cab of that truck as fast as I could. I was just in time, because the sky opened and the wind whipped the rain across the windshield in sheets.

"Better get out of here before we get stuck," he said. "You can come back and help me haul the wood out later if you'd like to make some more money."

I grinned and nodded.

The rumble of thunder and the beat of the rain were soothing as we drove home. I was thankful that he hadn't forgotten me, and I was thankful that he didn't forget to give me my money before he let me out in front of my house.

As I ran toward the door, I didn't care what Mom had for supper. I knew it would taste wonderful. The storm had settled in for the night, and that was exactly what I did after I ate. My bed never felt better, and thoughts of that approaching storm and the dark woods drifted away as I drifted off to sleep. I'd forgotten how good it was to be home.

Granny's Helper

I did not always get to spend my nights sleeping peacefully in my own bed. For a period of time, Granny Brown lived in a little house beside ours. She didn't like to stay by herself at night, so we older children took turns sleeping at her house to keep her company. We also helped by taking her supper, keeping her fire going, and winding up her Victrola, an old-time phonograph, so she could hear her records.

The trouble with being granny's helper was her early bedtime. And when she went to bed, she expected whoever was staying with her to go to bed, too. That was hard to do when I knew that right next door, my family was watching "The Lone Ranger" or "I Love Lucy." I tried to read comic books, but she'd tell me to turn out the light and go to sleep.

One night when I was staying with her, she told me she thought she was catching a cold. Granny kept a bottle of whiskey in her cabinet for medicinal purposes, so she had me bring her the bottle and a spoon. She took one spoonful, told me to take the bottle and spoon back to the kitchen, and then she turned over and went to sleep.

For some reason, I could not go to sleep that night. I'd close my eyes, but they'd pop open like they were on a spring. I thought, *What if I'm catching a cold like granny? That whiskey made her go right off to sleep. Maybe it would put me to sleep, too, if I took a little taste.*

I turned the covers back and slipped quietly out of bed. I tiptoed to the cabinet and took out the bottle of whiskey. I opened it and took a whiff. It burned my nose, so I figured it would be good for me. I didn't bother with a spoon. I turned up the bottle and took a sip. Immediately began to cough and sputter.

Granny woke up.

"What are you doing?" she called.

"I'm getting a drink of water," I answered. "My throat was tickling."

That part wasn't a lie. I was getting a drink of water at that point to try to sooth my throat.

"Get back in bed and don't fan the covers," she told me. "I don't want you getting sick!"

By now, my throat was no longer burning. In fact, it felt pretty good. I went back to bed like granny told me, but I decided to take the bottle with me. If one sip made me feel good, a couple more would probably make me feel better. I propped up in bed and downed two more swigs.

Gulp! Gulp!

These went down easier, and I began to feel warm.

Gulp! Gulp!

I was feeling better and better!

I don't know how long I sat propped up or how many more swigs I took before the room seemed to be moving. I put the bottle on the floor by the bed and slid down under the covers. I had no trouble sleeping now. I was out like a light.

When I woke, it was daylight. Daylight had never been painful before, but it was this morning. When I opened my eyes, the sun's rays seemed to be poking them like pins. Something else was poking me, too. I managed to keep my eyes open long enough to see granny and my dad standing over me. Dad was holding something in his hand.

Slowly, I remembered the events of the night before. I knew I had put the bottle down beside the bed. But I had meant to put it back in the cabinet before Dad came to wake us up for breakfast. Breakfast! My stomach turned at the thought of food.

"What's the meaning of this, son?" Dad asked, holding up the bottle.

I opened my eyes wide enough to see that there wasn't a great deal of whiskey left in it.

"Come on! Get up!" he ordered. "I want to know what happened here!"

I could see Granny behind him glaring at me. I didn't know if she was more concerned about me or her whiskey.

I moved the covers back and tried to sit up, but it suddenly seemed to me that my head was the size of a barrel. The room spun around and around and my head throbbed like a drumbeat. I lay back against the pillows. Wishing my head would go ahead and explode and get it over with. No such luck. It kept right on throbbing. I never felt such pain!

By now my mother had come over to see why we were not coming over to breakfast. When she saw me, she thought I had a normal illness.

"Law me, child! What's the matter?" she asked, looking from me to Dad and Granny.

"The little sneaking thing drank my whiskey," Granny tattled. "That's what's the matter! He needs a good whipping!"

The two started discussing my fate in loud, shrill voices, but my head was hurting too much to process what they were saying. Dad took pity on me and helped me out of bed and into my clothes. He half led and half carried me across the yard to our house, with Mom and Granny ranting and raving right at our heels. I skipped breakfast and school, and spent the day thinking I would never live to see another one.

Finally my headache eased off and my head felt like it was back to its normal size. Eventually food stayed down and life returned to normal.

In spite of Mom and Granny's recommendations about a whipping, my dad didn't spank me. He figured, and he was right, that I had punished myself more than he could. To this day, I still do not care for the taste of whiskey!

Cheers!

Even though, I gave up whiskey, I found that beer was a drink I could love. My wife didn't like the taste of it, but she didn't mind if I drank it. Once when we went to visit her parents in Russell County, I decided to take along a six-pack since it was a dry county.

My mother-in-law did not approve of drinking, so I thought it would not be a good idea for her to know that I brought the beer. It was a matter of respect. It was her house and I didn't want to offend her by breaking any of her rules.

"She won't mind your bringing a six-pack," my wife told me. "She just doesn't want anybody getting drunk."

"I can sneak it in," I said, "and she'll never know."

"Oh, I wouldn't try that," my wife warned. "She doesn't like anything sneaked on her. In fact, I don't think my sister and I ever sneaked anything and got away with it in our lives."

"Well, just watch me!" I said smugly.

My wife just looked at me and gave a little chuckle.

"I'm telling you, she has a sixth sense or something," she said. "She'll catch you for sure."

"We'll see," I said, and I put the six-pack in the trunk behind our luggage. My wife said nothing else.

When we arrived, my mother-in-law had company. She and a neighbor lady were sitting on the front porch visiting, so I thought it would be a good time to sneak my beer inside. My plan was to wait until everybody had gone to bed and then sneak a can in the freezer to cool for a few minutes. That way, I'd have a good cold beer before I went to sleep.

I was near the side porch by my mother-in-law's flowerbed, when I heard the neighbor say she had to go home. I heard the two women get up and I knew they could probably see me when they walked toward the drive, which was also by the side of the house.

I knew I couldn't make it to the door in time to get inside to hide my beer, so I quickly set it down among the flowers. They were tall, so, thank goodness, the beer was not visible. I stood there waiting for my mother-in-law to say goodbye and go inside.

When the neighbor got to the driveway, my mother-in-law suddenly called, "Wait a minute! Come see my flowers!"

Both women walked to the flowerbed where I was guarding my stash and stood there admiring the flowers. I held my breath until they finally turned and walked away and left my six-pack undiscovered.

While they were walking down the drive, I grabbed the beer and hurried inside. I took it directly to the bedroom and figured I was home free! I hid it inside the closet and figured I would now have no trouble putting my original plan into action that night.

The evening was uneventful. We had supper and sat around talking until bedtime. It was cloudy and a few flashes of lightning in the distance promised a summer storm later that night.

"I guess we should turn in," my mother-in-law said. "It may get stormy later."

I knew that if the storm looked severe, she'd make us all go down to the storm cellar until it was over.

We said goodnight and went to our rooms. I waited until everyone was asleep and I got quietly out of bed. I opened the closet, got out a can of beer, and started to the kitchen.

"Where are you going?" my wife whispered.

"I'm going to put this can in the freezer and let it cool for a few minutes," I whispered back.

"You will never get away with it," she said.

"She's asleep," I said. "She'll never know."

I crept to the kitchen, put my can of beer in the freezer, and tiptoed back to our room. I heard low thunder, but it didn't seem threatening. I figured we would not have to go to the cellar. That was a good thing. We would be able to sleep in our own beds.

Several minutes passed and I figured the beer was cold, I knew I'd better go get it out of the freezer before I went to sleep and let it freeze and burst. I'd never to be able to explain that.

I crept back to the kitchen. The thunder was still a long way off. It would probably just be a gentle rain and a good night to sleep. We could use a good storm to cool the air.

I opened the refrigerator door and started to open the freezer when the back door suddenly opened and a figure entered the room. I jumped and closed the refrigerator door.

Before I could speak, my mother-in-law, said, "I didn't mean to startle you. I couldn't remember if I closed the cellar door or not, so I thought I'd better go check."

"Yeah," I stammered. "It sounds like we might get some rain. I was just getting some water."

"That would taste good," she said. "But your cold beer in the freezer would probably taste better!"

With that she left me standing in the kitchen. From our bedroom, I heard my wife giggle.

The Chipmunk Saga

Of course my being outsmarted about the beer by my mother-in-law wasn't the only time I was outsmarted. And it certainly wasn't the only time my wife laughed at me about it. This time it was chipmunks.

When my wife and I moved to our Middletown home, our yard was full of wildlife. My wife thought the cutest residents were the chipmunks. I had to admit that they were cute, but when I stored some nuts in the garage and found them missing, I put the chipmunks at the top of my list of suspects. They were not as endearing as they had been after I had to buy mixed nuts at the store.

"Those little rascals stole my nuts," I accused. "We need to relocate them. They could find their own nuts in the park!"

"You mean trap them and take them away?" my wife asked, horrified.

"There are people that do that," I said. "The animals aren't hurt."

"No way!" my wife declared, coming to the chipmunks' defense. "This is their home. They were here first. Besides, I love the little things."

I nixed the removal idea, and we had a temporary truce.

Then I began to notice the little holes in the yard. The chipmunks dug tunnels, of course, and I began to imagine our entire house just collapsing into this great chipmunk tunnel system someday. Maybe it wasn't too late to save the house and my skin if I could just persuade them to leave on their own.

I began my campaign the day I noticed one of their holes right by the basement window off our patio. I must admit, I got off to a bad start.

I pulled out the garden hose and headed for the hole just as my wife looked out the window.

"What are you doing?" she asked, with a hint of suspicion in her voice.

I decided to tell her the truth. It was now or never.

"Those pesky chipmunks are undermining the foundation of our house," I told her. "I am going to flood 'em out."

"It will never work!" she said. "They will just move to another tunnel."

I didn't answer, but directed my energy to the project at hand. My wife came out and stood watching as I put the nozzle of the hose into the hole and turned the water on full force. Then I stood back satisfied and waited for the desired result. Nothing happened. We both stood there waiting a little longer. Still nothing.

"That's a lot of water," my wife commented quietly. "I wonder where it's going."

For some reason, a warning bell went off in my head.

Where was all that water going??

I turned off the faucet and looked around. The hole was close to the basement window, but surely no water went down there.

We rushed down the basement steps, and I saw my worst fear was a reality. The entire corner of the basement under the window was flooded! Somewhere there was a leak! I spent the rest of the afternoon mopping up water and sealing the leak. I put the hose away and thought I had put the entire unfortunate episode behind me. I returned from work the next day to see a little sign on the patio:

> *Dear Lonnie,*
> *Thanks for the indoor pool!*
> *Love,*
> *Chippie*

"Very funny," I told my wife, but she swore she had nothing to do with it.

I had thought of another way to keep the little critters at bay, so I went straight to the garage and got a piece of wood left over from the deck and placed it over the hole by the patio.

I left for work the next morning confident that they wouldn't be on the patio again. As I came in from work, I saw a little furry creature scurry off the wood and disappear into the grass. Lo and behold, there was another little sign on the patio:

> *Dear Lonnie,*
> *Thanks for the sun deck!*
> *Love,*
> *Chippie*

I could see my wife giggling at the window as I pulled up the little sign and put it in the garbage with the other one. I went out and bought a little sign for the patio that said

CHIPMUNK CROSSING

It was an act of complete surrender.

That was over twenty years ago. Generations of chipmunks have come and gone, but our house is still standing. I admit I must have been wrong about it falling into the tunnels.

But there is one strange thing you won't believe. Some nights, I go out on the patio at an unexpected time, and I see a little furry circle in the moonlight. Before they scatter into the night, I catch some tiny voices passing on the story of how their ancestors struggled against a man named Lonnie to keep their territory!

Excuses, Excuses!

Lots of us have things happen to us that we neither expect nor deserve. We are simply victims of circumstances. Such a thing happened to me on an icy winter morning in the nineties.

My wife and I woke as usual to get ready for work. Like many folks, even though we had a garage, we filled it with junk and left our cars parked in the driveway. That was a regrettable thing we did that night, because the locks on the car doors were frozen that morning.

My wife taught in a school across town, so she left before me in the mornings. I managed to open the door of her car without too much difficulty and started it up for her. By the time she dressed and had breakfast, the windshields were defrosted and the car was toasty warm. She kissed me goodbye, told me to be careful, and was off to work.

I finished reading the paper and decided I'd better go start my car so it could warm up. I wish I had heeded my wife's words about being careful, but I didn't. I did at least put on my work jacket before going out in the cold.

First, I tried the front door on the driver's side. It wouldn't budge. I tried the back door on the driver's side. It was frozen solid, too. I circled the car and tried the doors on the passenger side. No luck there either. I went inside and got a bucket of cold water. It didn't work on the driver's front door, but I finally opened the back one.

I crawled inside the car, reached over the seat, and inserted the key in the ignition. I realized I had a small problem. I had to push the accelerator down before my car would start, so I moved my right arm down to try to push it. My fingers wouldn't touch it from my position, so I leaned forward and shifted my weight. Then that unexpected, undeserved thing happened. I lost my balance and pitched forward on the console. I tried to break my fall, but I only succeeded in turning enough to land on my right arm, neatly wedging myself between the bucket seats. I couldn't turn either way, and I couldn't get any leverage to raise myself up.

I kicked my feet in the air, but they touched nothing solid. I was a little concerned now because my work jacket was light, and I was beginning to get cold. I looked hopefully out the car windows to see if a neighbor might be up and about, but all the houses were dark. I couldn't reach the horn or the accelerator. I was stuck and there was nothing I could do about it. My wife would probably find me frozen to death when she got home. I lay there alternating between panic and despair.

Finally, as the sun came up, my spirits began to rise, too. I would not give up without a fight. I did an inventory to see what parts of my body I could actually move. I found very few. I began to rock myself from side to side. Finally, I felt myself move a bit. I kept shaking and the car was shaking, too. It must have been a curious sight to anyone who might have driven by, because I was not visible to the outside.

I wiggled in that car for the next hour until I was finally able to turn enough to free myself. For the first time, I arrived at work an hour and a half late. I decided that honesty was the best policy, so I didn't make up any excuses. I told my boss and co-workers the truth. After they stopped laughing, they actually believed me. My boss said nobody would ever make up an excuse like that.

My wife wondered if she should get a sitter to stay with me in the mornings, but she settled for making sure my car doors were unlocked before she left for work.

Sweet Hour of Prayer

When somebody makes fun of me, I consider the possibility that I might be getting paid back for laughing at someone else. I am thinking of one person in particular. In my defense, I must say that I was just a kid at the time and I didn't mean any harm. In fact, the lady may never have known that my friends and I were laughing at her.

Miss Beatrice was one of the most dedicated members of the little neighborhood country church that we all attended. She was a very large woman who sat on the front pew and sang loudly, slightly off key with as much volume as she could muster. Believe me, it was a lot. She could drown out almost any other voice in church. A large number of the members mistook loud volume for quality voice control, and they said she was the best alto singer they ever heard. To this day, some of us can't hear "I've Got That Joy,

Joy, Joy Down In My Heart" without cringing from the memory of those singing sessions.

Miss Beatrice prayed with as much gusto as she used in singing. Looking back, I don't doubt her sincerity for a moment. I am sure she was a good Christian woman who uttered her prayers from the heart. Frankly, my friends and I didn't care about her sincerity or her heart. We loved to hear her pray for another reason, and we could hardly wait for altar call when everyone went down toward the altar and knelt on their knees to ask God's blessing. We made sure we had a good view of Miss Beatrice. She always made a fashion statement like no other.

In those days, money and clothing material were scarce. Companies that packaged food for cattle, and companies that sold flour and sugar would put the products in sacks that could be made into clothes and pillowcases. The sacks with designs were used for outer clothing like shirts, skirts, and dresses. Plain sacks would be used for pillowcases or slips or bloomers. The plain sacks often had the name of the product contained in them stamped on them, but it didn't matter because they were all hidden anyway.

Like most women, Miss Beatrice made her clothes from the sacks. Being modest, she made the legs of her bloomers a little long so she was well covered. Her skirts and dresses hit about mid-calf on her legs, and that was fine most of the time. We watched for the one time in church when fashion was very revealing.

Keep in mind that Miss Beatrice was a large woman. When the sermon ended, it was time to pray for sinners. The majority of the men stayed outside, so the front of the church was filled with woman who knelt to pray. The choir sang *Sweet Hour of Prayer* as the predominately female congregation left us children sitting in the pews and took their positions in front of the altar.

I guess Miss Beatrice was uncomfortable to hunker down because she would get on her knees and lean forward, bringing her rump up into the air enough to make her dress ride up. Of course, that left the bottom of her bloomers exposed. Nothing else was exposed, but we weren't looking for any sight of the flesh anyway. When she turned up her bottom to pray, right across her bottom was the name of the product that had once been in the sack from which she made the bloomers: BROWN SUGAR.

My friends and I could not contain ourselves at the sight of this spectacle. We snickered, giggled, and shook with laughter. After a couple of Sundays, my mom figured out what was going on. If we managed to get a good look and start to giggle, Mom would rise from prayer, yank us outside, call us little heathens, and leave us with our fathers before she went back inside,

where I'm sure she said a special prayer for our
souls.

Radio Active

My friends and I were not bad kids. We didn't mean to do anything wrong or upset people. We were typical boys looking for adventure and a good time. I always had an abundance of ideas for both, and my friends were always happy to join in. They often had the skills I didn't have to make some of my ideas materialize, so we were a good team. One such idea almost got us into a lot of trouble.

One of our favorite pastimes was to listen to the radio. We had a couple of radio stations in the area, so we had opportunities to visit and observe what was going on. Some of the musicians who had live programs on these stations made public appearances in towns near us. I played guitar, so I liked to go hear the bands. My friends just went along to enjoy the show.

One day when I was listening to a local broadcast, it occurred to me that it would be fun to have our own radio station. I mentioned this to my friends A.G. and Jerry, and they agreed with me. Jerry and I were good at organizing and programming, but AG was the whiz in the technical areas.

A.G.'s house was near a place called 'Possum Trot Hollow,' which was centrally located between my house and Jerry's. We agreed that this would be a good place for our base of operations. Of course, we needed a building for our station and A.G.'s father's old corncrib proved the perfect answer to our need. It was about forty feet from the barn where there was an electrical outlet. Our large extension cord would reach there easily from the corncrib.

Jerry and I were good at construction, so we set about adapting the corncrib to suit our needs. We divided the room into two areas. We put in a window in our control booth, just like we had seen in the real stations, with a worktable on each side. Soon we were ready for the technical installations. We had turntables that would play 78, 331/3, and 45 records, but we needed some supplies that we could only purchase at an actual store. We had some money we'd saved up from odd jobs, so we pooled our resources and went to Roy's TV and Repair Shop in town.

Roy sold us necessary things like a transmitter, microphone, outlet wiring, and such, but he didn't understand that we were actually going to build an active radio station. He told us the weather would affect how far our range would be, but he was sure we could reach out for a mile or two.

We took the purchases back to our station and A.G. installed them. We built our own antennae and brought records from our own personal collections. We assigned ourselves various jobs. A.G. was the engineer. I was the disc jockey and announcer who read commercials. (We advertised Kerns Bread, not because they sponsored us, but because that was the kind of bread we ate.) Jerry gave weather forecasts and sports and helped me with the announcing and programming. We set our "on air" hours from 4 PM to 6 PM because we couldn't get there until 4 PM after school and we had to be home for supper right after 6 PM. We scrambled our initials and came up with ABRG as our call letters, and we were in business.

We were really smart kids to be able to set up our own radio station, but we weren't smart enough to know that we had to have assigned frequencies, a license to operate, and other things like that. We knew nothing of government commissions and agencies that had authority such things. Ignorance was bliss for a while.

We could hardly wait for school to end each day. Jerry and I would hop on our bikes and peddled as fast as possible to A.G.'s house. Our opening theme each day was *Poor People of Paris* by Chet Atkins. From then until sign-off time at 6 PM, we filled the airways with music, news, and sports, with a few commercials thrown in.

As days passed, we varied our program a bit. I would take my guitar and play live on the radio. Mom found purely by trial and error that we could be heard on the radio if she turned the dial as far as possible to the end. She and Dad and the neighbors began to listen and enjoy our presentations.

One afternoon right in the middle of a broadcast, a bee decided to pay us a visit. I was in the middle of introducing a record when the bee buzzed by my head.

I swatted at it and it only made it angry.

BUZZ! It came like a dive-bomber right at my head! I ducked, but I knew it would circle back.

"Get that damn bee out of here," I yelled, afraid it was going to sting me.

"You just said that on the air," Jerry whispered. "You are not allowed to curse on the radio!"

That scared me worse than the bee! I knew someone would come to get me. I worried about that for days, but nothing happened. Not then, anyway!

We didn't broadcast on Saturday, so we boys were out pursuing other adventures when trouble came looking for us in the form of a government investigator. Since we weren't around, he talked to A.G.'s mother.

"We have reports of an illegal transmitter somewhere between Russell Springs and Columbia," he told her. "It's interfering with the frequencies from the local radio stations. We've traced it here and I've come to shut it down and find the responsible parties."

"The boys have a little station they play around with up there on the hill," she said. "They don't mean to interfere with anything, though."

"Mind if I take a look?" he asked.

"Why, no. Go on," she said.

He came back totally amazed.

"How old are these boys?" he asked.

She told him our ages as near as she knew.

"It's a good thing they are not 21," he said. "They could be in big trouble for an operation like this. I'd like to talk to the boys."

Since we were nowhere to be found, he left with the promise from A.G.'s mother that the station would be dismantled immediately and that there would be no more broadcasts. We were three sad boys when we had to carry out that order, but we were a little proud that a government official had been so impressed with our abilities.

Later when I became a professional musician and played with name bands on major radio and television stations, I never experienced as big a thrill as I did when I played on ABGR on 'Possum Trot Ridge.

The Haunted Smith Woods

Sometimes things happened that brought us chills instead of chuckles. Most of the time when something strange occurred, we could come up with a logical explanation, but it was the small percentage of times when we couldn't find an answer that left us wondering. My friends, my brothers and sisters, and I loved to hear our parents tell these stories.

My mom grew up in Adair County in the 1200-acre Smith Woods, named after a man who settled there back in the 1800's. It was common knowledge that strange sounds could be heard in the dark shadows among the trees. There were numerous reports of hogs squealing or babies crying in there at night, but searchers turned up nothing. Hogs did run loose sometimes back then, so, even though nobody found them, they could actually have been there and ran off from the searchers. The babies crying could have been squirrels, because they sometimes made funny sounds like a baby. But there were other things that couldn't be explained away so easily.

One such incident happened to my mom, two of her sisters, and their mother. It was a bright sunny day when they decided to go pick blueberries that grew wild on the banks along the old wagon road.

The wagon road was a simple dirt road with ruts worn deep from much travel. It was only wide enough for one wagon with no room for pedestrians. In several places, the banks on both sides were so high that anyone caught walking in those locations had to scramble up the banks to safety if the horses and wagon happened along at the same time.

There was nothing in sight along the road, and not a scary thought in the heads of my mom and her companions as they walked to the spot where the blueberries grew in abundance. They were chattering happily and filling their buckets when they heard a wagon coming. They could hear the horses snorting and the wagon wheels squeaking over the bumps in the road

"Hurry and climb up the bank," my grandmother instructed. "We need to get out of the way."

She and the girls scurried up the bank and sat down to see who was going to pass by. Even though the sounds continued distinctly for a minute or two, nothing appeared. Then they stopped altogether. Mom and the others stood up and looked around, but there was no wagon or horses in sight. Puzzled, they even walked down the road a bit, but nothing ever came in sight.

My dad had a similar experience when he and a neighbor were working in a cornfield beside that same road. The sun was beaming down, and chopping corn had left them hot and sweaty.

They took a short break to rest and lean against their hoes.

They were just standing there talking when they noticed a man wearing a suit coming up the road. That was unusual for a number of reasons. First of all, it was too hot to be wearing a suit. And second, it was not the custom to wear a suit except to church on Sunday or to a funeral. It wasn't Sunday, and as far as they knew, nobody had died. They watched him approached and turned back to start hoeing, thinking he'd come on by and say hello. They'd hoed only a hill or two of corn when they realized that he hadn't come on by yet. They looked up and he was nowhere in sight.

"Where did he go?" the neighbor asked Dad.

"I don't know," said Dad. "Maybe he passed out from the heat and fell down."

They stepped to the road where they could see more clearly, but there was no sign of him. He would not have had time to walk out of sight because they could see a good way in all directions. He had simply vanished.

We began to think that maybe the Smith Woods was a portal where people could walk in and out to another time.

Uncle Buck swore he met something that shouldn't have been there as he was coming home one night.

Uncle Buck bought himself a retired racehorse, but he needed a new bridle for it. He rode the horse out to the country store and made his purchase just before dark one night. Of course he talked a bit with the store's owner and some of the men gathered there, so it was dark when he started back home.

The ride was uneventful until Uncle Buck neared a little branch that ran out of the Smith

Wood's and crossed the road. The moon was out, so the road and the branch were visible. Just as the horse carried Uncle Buck near the little stream, something suddenly rose shimmering in the air and hovered over the road in front of the horse. Uncle Buck saw it clearly for a few seconds before his horse reacted. It looked exactly like a leopard skin! Of course, Uncle Buck knew there were no leopards in Kentucky, and if there had been, they would not rise from a stream and float in the air.

The horse knew it, too, and it wasn't about to stay around to figure out what it was. It reared in the air and threw Uncle Buck to the ground. Then it put its talent to use and raced home.

Uncle Buck discovered he was pretty good at running himself because he got home not too long after the horse arrived.

When he saw the thing the last time, it was still floating by the branch above the road near

Smith's Woods. He never knew what it was, where it came from, or where it went.

Other Unexplained Encounters

After Mom and Dad married, they rented a house not too far away from the Smith's Woods area from Mr. Brock. Since Mom and Dad didn't need the barn space, Mr. Brock kept his tobacco hanging in there after it was cut, until it was stripped and taken to market.

One night Mom and Dad were awakened from a sound sleep by a terrible ruckus in the barn.

"What in the world is that?" Mom asked.

"I sounds like hogs fighting," Dad answered.

"But we don't have any hogs," Mom said.

"Maybe some got loose and got into the barn," Dad said. "I'd better go see."

"Wait for me, "Mom said. "And get your gun."

Dad took the gun, and he and Mom proceeded to the barn to see what was going on. The sounds got louder as the approached, and they were definitely coming from inside the barn. Dad opened the door and they peered inside. The noise immediately stopped. They looked around, but discovered no sign of any animals. Except for the tobacco, the barn was empty.

Many nights during the time they lived there, this experience would be repeated. They checked it out a few more times, but finally, they just stopped going.

Dad learned later that Mr. Brock had butchered hogs there many years before. Maybe it was those ghost hogs they heard before they were slaughtered.

It was at this same house that I had my first brush with the supernatural when I was just a baby.

There was a little boxed room at the back of the house, with windows on both sides and the back that looked out over a little cemetery down the road. If the windows were left open, a cool breeze usually blew through and made that room cooler than the others. Mom liked to put me in there to nap if I was fussy, because the cool breeze seemed to sooth me.

One night, Aunt Mary and Uncle Charlie came for supper. After they ate, Mom put me on the bed in that little room to sleep while they all moved to the front porch while the house cooled after the fire in the kitchen cook stove.

I didn't sleep long, though. They had just settled in to visit on the porch when I began to cry. It wasn't a fussy cry like I cried when I just wanted attention. I cried loudly as though I was really frightened or sick. Mom started to go get me, but Aunt Mary stopped her.

"I'll get him," she told Mom. "You rest. You just cooked supper over that hot stove."

Aunt Mary said that when she entered the room, it was unusually cool for such a warm might. I was kicking and screaming, so she went straight to the bed and picked me up. As I snuggled against her shoulder, I was still shaking. She tried to sooth me, but then it happened. An icy cold hand touched her arm!

She said it was a wonder she didn't drop me, but she held on and raced from the room, through the house, and out on the porch. When she told what happened, Dad and Uncle Charlie checked the room and all around the house, but nobody was there.

A woman in the neighborhood and her baby had died a few days before in childbirth. Maybe her ghost came back and thought I was her baby.

One of our neighbors named Jim swore he had a ghostly encounter not far from there. He and his friend Marvin liked to get together with some other guys they knew and drink moonshine and gamble until the wee hours of morning. They had been indulging in these two vices one night, so it was late when they were riding their horses home on the road that led by the country church and cemetery where a neighbor, Aunt Fetney Ann as everybody called her, had just been buried. Even though people whispered she was a witch, she was allowed to be buried on sacred ground in the graveyard near the road. Just as they rode past, they heard a funny yelp near her tombstone.

"What was that?" asked Marvin.

The moonshine had Jim feeling pretty brave and a wee bit disrespectful of the dead.

"That's just old Aunt Fetney Ann after a frog for one of her spells," he called back to Marvin, laughing.

The words were barely out of his mouth, when something jumped on the back of his horse and grabbed him around the neck. Jim said it was the coldest thing he ever felt. It chilled his bones. He couldn't turn around far enough to see what it was. He tried to shake it off, but it hung on.

Marvin was behind, but he could only see a shadowy form. He couldn't get close enough to tell what it was because his horse reared straight up and refused to go forward an inch.

Jim's horse took off at breakneck speed.

"Whoa!" Jim yelled, pulling on the reins. "Whoa!"

The horse ignored him and flew on down the road. When they reached a place where the road crossed a little creek, the thing on Jim's back turned loose and leapt off. By the time Jim got his horse stopped, the thing was gone without a trace.

Jim never saw anything like it again, but then, he was never disrespectful to the dead after that either.

Witch Tales

We had our share of witch tales, but two stand out in my mind. We never really believed in witches, but there were two old women who definitely made us wonder.

One old woman, whom everybody called a witch, lived down the road from Mom and Dad a few years after they were married. Mom never had much to do with her. They would speak and pass, and not bother each other.

Then Mom decided to raise some little chickens. They were thriving just fine until the old woman came by one day and asked Mom to sell her some of them. Mom explained that she didn't have any to sell, but the old woman didn't like that answer.

"If you won't let me have them, then you won't enjoy them either. Something will come along and cut their heads off," she warned, and stomped off down the road.

Mom was shocked at the old woman's response. There were plenty of places to buy chickens, so there was no reason for mom to sell hers to the old woman.

Mom fixed supper and finally put the episode out of her mind. When she got up the next morning, she went out to feed her chickens. Every one of them was lying near the hen house with their heads cut off. Even though there were weasels and foxes around, it didn't look like animals had attacked them. The heads looked like they had been cut off instead of bitten.

Was it just a coincidence? We never knew. But Mom didn't try to raise any more chickens until they moved to another place.

The other woman who was considered a witch was old Mrs. Eliza. Her husband was long dead, but she had a daughter who married and lived in the community not too far from her mother. She and her mother were like day and night. The mother had a mean, grumpy disposition, but the daughter was sweet and friendly.

It was said that Mrs. Eliza could and would cast spells on anyone who displeased her. Children ran away if they came upon her gathering herbs or rocks when they were out playing. People said she used these things in spells.

One man in our community had the misfortune of falling out of her good graces. His name was Mr. Miller and he worked as a hired hand to all the neighbors. His mind was slow, but he was a good worker. Employers were happy to pick him up and take him home since he had no means of transportation to and from work.

His strong point was definitely not scheduling. He never wanted to hurt anybody's feeling, so he'd promise to work for several people on the same day. The person who arrived first in the morning to get him was the one who had his services for the day. The others were out of luck. Some of them did not take this lightly. One was old Mrs. Eliza.

She had hired him to plow her garden because she was anxious to get it planted before the rain set in. He'd promised faithfully to be there on the appointed day. Morning came and went, but he didn't. Mrs. Eliza finally went to see if he was sick, but she learned he was off working for somebody else. She left muttering to herself.

That day, Mr. Miller's employer for the day brought him home early with a terrible headache. He took immediately to his bed because his pain was so severe. He lived near the country store, so word spread fast about how much he was suffering. The neighbors came with every home remedy they could think of, but nothing helped. He could not keep down food or water. They called in the doctor, but he was as unsuccessful as the others in treating the poor man. His agony continued for three days.

On the third day, Mrs. Eliza's daughter came to the store for supplies and heard what had happened. She went to visit Mr. Miller and watched for just a minute. Then she headed toward her mother's house with a very determined look on her face. Two neighbors tagged along to see what would happen. She didn't seem to mind. Maybe she was even unaware of their presence. She went straight to her mother and confronted her.

"Mother, I want you to remove that spell from Mr. Miller," she said.

"There is no spell," replied Mrs. Eliza.

"Yes, there is," said the daughter. "That poor man is going to die if something isn't done. Remove it!"

"No!" said Mrs. Eliza.

The daughter stepped close to her mother, reached down, and yanked up her long skirt. Something was clearly tied in the hem of her petticoat.

"Remove them now!" ordered the daughter.

Mrs. Eliza hesitated a second and then bent down and untied the hem. Out fell three smooth pebbles!

"Satisfied?" sneered the old woman.

"Yes," her daughter answered simply.

She and her mother looked at each other and the old woman went back inside. The young woman sat down and spoke to the neighbors who had come along for the first time.

"Let's sit down and rest a minute," she said.

They had sat there just long enough to catch their breath, when a neighbor came driving down the road and stopped.

"It's a miracle!" he shouted. "Mr. Miller's headache finally just stopped! He's going to be okay."

Was it a miracle or magic? Old Mrs. Eliza was the only one who ever knew for sure!

A Goat To Note

Perhaps the story that fascinated me most of all happened to old Mr. Wilson at a farm he bought several miles from us.

It started when Mr. Wilson moved into his new place. He went out to milk the first night, and a very annoying goat came into the barn and started butting at the cows.

"Get out of here," Mr. Wilson ordered, but the goat was very persistent.

Mr. Wilson had to stop milking, chase the goat out of the barn, and calm the cows before he could finish.

"Does our neighbor have a goat?" he asked his wife when he went inside.

"I don't think so," she said. "At least I haven't seen one. Why?"

"Well, somebody must have one. When I was milking, one came in and started butting at the cows," he explained.

"I'm going over to the neighbor's house in the morning," she said. "I heard that they sell eggs and I need some. I'll see what I can find out."

She came back the next morning with some news.

"Our neighbors haven't had a goat since their daughter disappeared a few years ago. She had one as a pet, but it died not long after she came up missing. They never got another one."

"Well somebody's got one. It was in our barn last night," he said.

They thought no more about it until Mr. Wilson went to milk that night. He looked up and saw the goat again, and they went through the same routine they had gone through the night before.

"That dang goat was back!" he said, when he brought the milk inside.

Much to their amazement, the goat paid nightly visits for the next few days. Mr. Wilson finally had enough. When the goat came in and started butting, he chased it outside, but this time he followed it. He was determined to find out who owned it so he could speak to them about keeping it at home.

He was surprised when it headed to the back of one of the pastures that he owned. He followed and saw it stop at a pile of rocks in a fence corner. He moved quickly toward the rocks and the goat climbed on the rocks and just disappeared before his eyes. He moved the rocks and discovered a bone. He looked no further. He went straight to his house and called the sheriff.

They didn't have DNA testing back then, so they couldn't be sure the bones were human. The neighbors thought the search for their missing daughter was over, even though the killer was never caught. They thought the little goat might have been her little pet that wanted someone to know where she was. Once the bones were discovered, the little goat was never seen again.

Animals and Angels

Ghost animals didn't just appear to inform of someone's passing; they sometimes came to give other warnings or to give hopeful news.

It was a common belief where I grew up that if a bird flew into the house, it was a sign that someone in that household was going to die. There was never an explanation about why people died even if birds didn't fly inside, but it was held as a special sign of oncoming death anyway.

When the flu epidemic hit Kentucky back in the early 1900's, doctors were at a loss as to how to treat it. Even if they'd had medicine, it would still have been hard to get it to everybody because doctors were scarce in rural areas. There were no hospitals where they could bring all the sick people together, so the doctors had to travel from home to home. Sometimes they became ill themselves. Sometimes, entire families were wiped out and would all be lying dead in their homes at the same time. It was extremely hard to see little children suffer and die.

The White family was stricken with the deadly influenza, but they were beginning to recover. Their little boy was the weakest of all, but they saw signs that he was beginning to improve, too. His fever was down and he had eaten a little soup and managed to keep it down.

Then one night as Mr. White opened the door to go get fresh water from the spring, a white bird flew past him into the room. It circled around the boy's bed and fluttered at the window trying to get out. It finally flew back out the door.

That night, the little boy's fever rose again. In spite of all they did to try to help him, he was dead by morning. The family felt that the bird was an omen.

Another time, a bird brought a message of hope, and my mom was the one who heard the message.

A neighbor's little boy Ervin was sick. His Aunt Bessie had gone to church the night before, and stopped to tell Mom and her family how serious his condition was. She said the doctor thought he wouldn't live. Bessie asked everybody to pray for him. When she left for home, she looked pale and worried.

Mom thought about him when she went to bed that night. She thought of how she'd miss hearing him come across the fields yodeling and singing. She just couldn't picture him dead, and she said a prayer for his recovery.

Then Mom heard in her left ear the sound of a whippoorwill singing over and over, "He's gonna get well. He's gonna get well!" At that, she stopped worrying and went to sleep.

The next morning when she woke up, she told her family what she'd heard.

"He's gonna get well," she said. "I know he is!"

The family told her they hoped she was right, but that she must be prepared for the worst.

That weekend, little Ervin began to perk up. He just kept getting better and better, and his Aunt Bessie finally came to say he was all right. Death passed him by that time, and he went on to live a long, happy life.

Sometimes when Death was near, angels came to bring the message. That was what happened to Great-grandmother Rooks. She had been sick for a week and Mom's sister Carrie was staying with her.

One Saturday morning she said to Carrie, "Go get your mother. I want to tell her something."

Carrie couldn't imagine why she would send her home to get her mother, but she obeyed. Grandmother Rooks immediately went to see what her mother wanted.

"What is it, Mother?" she asked. "What did you want to tell me?"

"I saw something last night," she answered. "I wasn't dreaming when I saw it, and I wanted you to know."

"What was it?" Grandmother asked.

"Last night, I had just finished my prayers when I saw a little crippled angel dancing at the door. It's a sign I am going to die."

"You must have been dreaming," Grandmother told her. "Maybe you were thinking of our little crippled cousin in Missouri. Maybe it's a sign that we are going to hear from her."

"No, I wasn't dreaming," Great-grandmother Rooks insisted. "It was about me, and I want you to help me get my affairs in order."

"I think the angel could be a sign that you will be better," Grandmother insisted.

"No," said Great-grandmother Rooks. "The angel was crippled. It is a sign that I won't be healed."

Grandmother saw that it was useless to argue with her, so she decided to keep quiet.

To humor her, Grandmother stayed and helped her go through her things. She made note of who in the family was to get each of Great-grandmother's possessions. The next Saturday, Great-grandmother Rooks died peacefully in her bed. It was exactly a week after the little crippled angel had danced at her door.

Scary Tales

Some of the scary stories we heard were not warnings or answers to mysteries. When the work was done for the day, neighbors liked to gather at each other's houses and exchange stories. Some tellers swore their tales were true, but whether they were or not didn't matter. These were some of the best storytellers who ever lived and they provided many unforgettable evenings of shivery entertainment.

My Grandmother Sally had a ghostly encounter that she swore was true. It was several months after her mother had died, and it was the night of the "hook" moon. It was believed that this small "sliver" of a moon could pull the dead from their graves. Granny Sally was more concerned about the small amount of light it gave as she hurried home from a neighbor's house where she had gone to borrow some lard. She had to cook for field hands the next day and she wouldn't have time to go to the store. She had to start early because cooking was a new chore she'd had to take on since her mother died.

The path that led between the two farms dipped down into a little valley and was lined with trees. There was a spring beside the road where cool, clear water was plentiful. Lots of people stopped there to rest and get a drink of water.

As Granny Sally approached the spring, she could see someone sitting on a stump by the side of the road. Even though she was a little jittery because of the hook moon, she really was not expecting anything out of the ordinary.

When she neared the stump, she saw it was a woman sitting there with her head down. When she was right beside her, the woman looked up. Granny Sally said she was never so shocked in her life. She was literally too scared to move. Her dead mother was sitting on the stump looking up at her.

"How's the family, Sally?" she asked.

Granny Sally didn't answer. She said her brain must have told her feet to move, but she didn't remember sending the signal. She just realized she was flying down that road faster than she had ever run before.

When she reached the house, she was gasping for air. The family thought something awful had happened to her.

"What's the matter?" her father asked.

"Momma," she managed to say, and it was several minutes before she could tell them what happened. She said she had held on to that bucket of lard so tight that her father had to pry it out of her hands. She realized that her mother wouldn't hurt her, but she refused to go back through that stretch of road at night by herself again.

The Gold Tooth

My wife's great-grandfather, Christopher, was involved with a haunted tooth. Now I know that may sound funny, but it didn't turn out that way.

Christopher was married twice in his life, both times to women named Elizabeth. The name was all that was the same, because his treatment of the two women was quite different. The first Elizabeth was a woman who didn't smile much in the pictures passed down in the family. It could have been because she was unhappy or tired, or it could have been because she had a bad tooth.

The story goes that the first Elizabeth had a front tooth that was rotten and discolored, and she wanted her husband to get her a gold tooth. Gold teeth were quite stylish at the time. Most likely, she didn't smile in photographs because she didn't want the bad tooth to show.

Christopher could be quite stingy, and perhaps Elizabeth Number One could not be persuasive enough to change that characteristic. In any case, the poor woman died without getting her gold tooth.

Christopher later remarried and, of course, this was Elizabeth Number Two. The second Elizabeth was shown smiling in her pictures, and when she had trouble with a tooth, I guess she considered it a high priority to replace it so she could go on smiling. She, too, asked her husband for a gold tooth.

Nobody ever knew why Christopher was more generous with the second Elizabeth than he was with the first. Maybe the smile charmed him, or maybe the second wife was more demanding. Whatever the reason, Christopher gave in and got the tooth for the second wife. If he thought he had solved the problem, he was in for a shock. Trouble had just begun!

Elizabeth Number Two had just begun to enjoy her tooth, when a very odd, and annoying thing begin to happen. Christopher noticed that she always seemed to be messing with it— rubbing it, pushing on it—things like that.

"Does your tooth hurt?" he asked her.

"No," she said.

"What's wrong with it then?" he wanted to know. "You're always picking at it like it's bothering you."

"Nothing's wrong," she insisted.

Christopher let it go for a few days, but she just kept doing it. Finally he couldn't take it any longer.

"I want to know what's the matter!" he demanded.

Poor Elizabeth broke down and admitted that something was indeed very wrong.

"You'll think I'm crazy," she admitted. "But something tugs at my tooth all the time."

"What do you mean?" asked Christopher. "What could tug at your tooth?"

"That's the crazy part," she said. "When I sit down to eat, I see a shadowy form come down the stairs. It comes to me and tugs at the tooth. Then it vanishes."

"That is crazy!" said Christopher. "You must be imagining things. We'll have to go back and have that tooth fixed. It must not fit right."

He knew it wasn't like his wife to imagine things, though, and it was just a short time until he knew she was telling the truth.

They had sat down for their noon meal one day and Christopher was facing the stairs. He was amazed to see a shadow moving down the stairs—a shadow in the shape of a woman. It looked like someone he knew all too well—his first wife Elizabeth!

The ghostly figure moved to the table and reached out toward the mouth of the second Elizabeth.

Christopher jumped to his feet, knocking his chair over with a clatter!

"Good God!" he muttered, along with some other choice words, which caused the ghost to promptly vanish.

The first Elizabeth apparently had not taken kindly to the thought that he would buy a tooth for another woman when he wouldn't do it for her. Evidently, she thought that if she didn't deserve to have a new tooth, the second wife didn't either.

Her showing up was enough to spook Christopher, or maybe his conscience just bothered him. Either way, he announced to his second Elizabeth that they weren't going to share the house with the first one! They found a new place and moved.

The old place stood empty for a while. Then one night a fire broke out and it burned to the ground. Maybe the first Elizabeth got tired of being there alone and went out in a blaze of glory.

Damron's Creek

Christopher's daughter Fanny, my wife's grandmother, had some eerie experiences when she married and moved with her husband Mike to a little farmhouse on Damron's Creek.

They rented the house from Mrs. Withers, who lived in a house they could see across the field.

"I'll leave a light in my window so you can see it and come over if you get scared or need me," Mrs. Withers told Fanny. "I know your husband will work late sometimes."

Mike was a farmer, and he and the other farmers would help each other out with their crops when work had to be finished. Being alone didn't bother Fanny, though.

"That's nice of you, Mrs. Withers, but I'm not afraid to stay by myself," said Fanny.

"We'll see," smiled Mrs. Withers, but she didn't push the issue.

Several days passed that were uneventful. Mike went to work and Fanny unpacked and got settled in the new place. Mike finished work and came home for supper before sundown. Mrs. Withers was true to her word and kept the light in her window as she had promised. Fanny had to admit to herself that it was sort of comforting to see it glowing in the distance.

Then one night, clouds banked in the west, and Mike and the other farmers worked to finish the spring planting before the rain started. Dusk settled into darkness as the clouds moved closer. Fanny cooked supper and left the doors open to let the fresh breeze blow through and cool the house. As she lit her lamps, she looked across the field and saw the lamp burning brightly in Mrs. Withers' window. She smiled and thought to herself that she must go over to pay a friendly visit soon.

She sat down near the door to watch for Mike and wait for the rain to start. As the first drops rattled against the tin roof, she heard something else. Whispers! At first, she couldn't believe it.

"It's just the wind," she said to herself, but she knew it wasn't.

The whispers grew louder, but indistinct. She couldn't understand what they were saying. They seemed to be coming from different places in the room. Suddenly, she was filled with a fear like nothing she had ever felt before. She couldn't stand it. She had to get out of there.

She dashed out of the house and ran across the yard. The rain hit her face, but she didn't care. She didn't see Mike until she ran right into his arms. Then she sobbed out what had happened.

Back in the house, she put on dry clothes and she and Mike ate supper. Everything was quiet now.

"Maybe it was the wind I heard," she told him.

"I'm sure it was," he assured her. "There's nothing to be afraid of here."

More uneventful days passed and Fanny began to feel a little silly about the way she had reacted. It was more of a comfort now than ever, though, to see the light in Mrs. Withers' window.

Late one afternoon, Fanny decided to weed her flowerbeds. She worked until the sunset and it was just between daylight and dusk. She heard the rumble of low thunder, and she knew Mike would probably work late again to finish before the storm. She was about to go inside, when she heard someone walking toward her in the yard.

She saw by his shoes that it was a man. Then she noticed he was wearing a suit. She had thought it was Mike when she first heard the footsteps. She couldn't imagine who it could be. Men only wore suits to church or funerals. She stood up to greet her visitor—and saw that he had no head!

Fanny heard someone screaming, but she was half way across the field before she realized that someone was her.

"AHHHHH! AHHHH!"

When she reached Mrs. Withers' house, Mrs. Withers was already running to meet her.

"Come in," she said. "Tell me what's wrong."

"The man," was all Fanny could get out.

"Calm down," Mrs. Withers told her. "You're all right now. I'll fix you some tea."

As she drank the tea, Fanny told Mrs. Withers about the whispers and the man with no head. Oddly enough, the old lady did not seem surprised.

When Fanny finished, Mrs. Withers said, "You're not the first one that has happened to. That's why I left the light on for you to see."

"I don't understand," said Fanny. "Where did the whispers come from? Who was the man?"

"Nobody knows for sure," Mrs. Withers answered. "But I'll tell you what I know. There used to be moonshine stills all along the creek. When we bought the property, we heard stories about shootouts between the moonshiners and the revenuers. There was one awful tale about a government man getting his head blown off in one of the raids. Maybe the whispers come from the moonshiners when they were hiding, waiting for the revenuers to come."

Fanny and Mike found another place and moved. Fanny didn't want any more contact with whatever was there.

There are those of us who can't really believe that a headless man is walking around anywhere. We explain it away by saying it was a trick of the late, late afternoon light. All the same, I was always glad I never had cause to walk along the banks of Damron's Creek after dark!

Fears and Reality

Everything frightening wasn't always connected to the supernatural. We had our share of crimes and personal demons to deal with. Sometimes someone would be shot over a gambling debt or a boundary dispute. Some were tried in court and punished, while others escaped and were never caught. Some had mental problems, like one man who served in World II and hanged himself because he couldn't deal with the horrors of war.

I don't recall a bank ever being robbed, but some thieves did raid hen houses or break into smoke houses and steal hams. Mostly that happened during the Depression when people had no money for food and needed to feed their families.

That might have been the reason for a strange happening at my wife's house when she was just a little girl. Her family lived in a two-room log house on her grandmother's farm. There were beds in both rooms, but the bed in the kitchen was where my wife's sister, Teema, slept.

It was a warm summer night, and the family had gone to bed happy. Their father had sold some cattle that day, and there was money for some extra things they needed. It was a small community, so everybody knew when sales like that were made. It was also common knowledge that very few farmers like my wife's dad, Tom, ever put their money in the bank.

Tom had put up screen doors, so they left the main doors open when they slept. There were no air-conditioners then, so this was a way to make the house cooler and more comfortable for sleeping. Tom was a carpenter as well as a farmer, so he had put secure latches on the screen doors. The screen wire itself was very stiff and hard to cut.

Everybody was sound asleep when something woke Teema. She thought she'd been dreaming at first, but she heard it again. The moon was not full that night and, since they had no electricity, there were no outside lights. She listened and determined it was something at the back door. She thought it could be a raccoon, but as she grew fully awake, she knew it was no raccoon sound.

Wheet! Wheet! Wheet!

Then it dawned on her what it was! Someone was whittling by the latch. Someone was trying to get the door open!

Teema lay there terrified. She had never been able to scream loudly in her life, so she would never be able to make her dad hear her. She couldn't go wake him up because the kitchen door was between her and the door to the other room. She'd have to cross in front of the would-be intruder and she was afraid to do that. She lay there and continued to listen.

Wheet! Wheet! Wheet!

She realized she had to do something! She didn't know how long the whittling had gone on before it woke her! The person out there might be able to get inside any minute! She sat up in the bed, with the intention of getting up and dashing into the other room. Just then, she heard her dad cough and clear his throat. He was awake! He would hear her!

"Daddy, someone's breaking in!" she yelled as loudly as she could.

It was loud enough. She heard the bedsprings squeak as her dad jumped up and grabbed his gun.

The unknown whittler must have heard her or her dad, or maybe both. Teema immediately heard footsteps running away into the dark.

They woke her mom, too.

"What is it?" she asked, sitting up in bed.

"Somebody's outside trying to get in," she heard her dad say.

"I don't hear anything," her mom said.

By now Teema was up and in the doorway to the other room.

"There was somebody whittling at the door! I heard them!" Teema told her. "They ran off when Daddy got up!"

"Aw, you were just dreaming!" said her mom. "Go back to bed! We've got to get some sleep 'cause your daddy has to get up early and go to work tomorrow"

Tom wasn't so quick to brush it off as a dream, though.

"Let me check it out," he said.

He lit the lamp and looked at the door. Then he opened the door, reached down, and picked something up. By now everybody was up, gathered by the lamp. Tom opened up his hand and showed them a handful of wood shavings.

He went outside and looked all around, but nobody was to be found. He figured that whoever it was would not be back that night, so he told everybody it was safe to go back to bed.

The next morning, they saw tracks that headed toward the barn. Tom tried to follow the tracks, but they disappeared in the grass. Nobody came back to try it again.

Teema and Other Burglars

Teema had two other encounters with would-be burglars when she was a young woman. The first one was so funny that it took a long time to live it down.

She was home alone one night reading a book. By now she was living in a house with electricity. The family dog lived in a fenced-in back yard, but the little hound did not always choose to stay there. He'd often dig his way out and come around to the front door to see if he could persuade someone to let him in.

On this night, Teema was reading a book that had a shiny silver strip on the cover. She was distracted by a noise at the front door, and she assumed that the dog had dug out and come around again. With her book still in hand, she went to the door and opened it. The light from a lamp by the table reflected from the cover, making the book look somewhat like a weapon.

She heard a rustle in the bush by the door. She didn't see the little dog, but she called out loudly, "Come in, Honey! Come on in!"

There was another rustle just as she flipped on the porch light. Much to her amazement, something bolted and ran from the bushes—but it was a man, not the dog!!

We teased her for a long time about scaring a burglar away by inviting him in!

It wasn't long after that, that she had another encounter with a burglar in a bush. She had been visiting a young married couple, Arthur and Faye, and their young son Artie. As she started to leave, she saw a bush by the basement window and suddenly remembered her previous experience. She stopped and shook her finger at the bush.

"Arthur, you ought to cut that bush," she said. "If anybody wanted to break into your house, that would be a perfect place to hide."

"Yeah," Arthur agreed. "I've been meaning to do that."

Teema got in her car and drove away. When she got home, the phone was ringing. It was a very excited Arthur.

"Did you see what happened as you drove away?" asked Arthur.

"No," she said. "What?"

"A man jumped from behind that bush and ran down the street!"

She was as amazed as Arthur. Of course, several days passed and Arthur was busy with other things. He neglected to cut the bush.

One day Arthur was at work and Faye was vacuuming the house. When she got to the front entranceway, she suddenly remembered it was time to pick up her little son Artie from nursery school. She switched off the vacuum cleaner, picked up her purse and car keys from the hall table, got in her car in the driveway and drove off.

In a few minutes, she and Artie arrived home and she opened the front door. As they started in, Faye heard something moving in the basement. They had no pets, so she knew something was wrong. She thought of Teema's warning and that someone had been hiding behind the bush that night. She left the door open and hurried with Artie to the next-door neighbor's house, where they called the police.

The police responded quickly. They told Faye and Artie to stay with the neighbor until they searched the house. In a few minutes, the police came out with a man in handcuffs.

One of the officers came over and told Faye they had captured a burglar! He admitted that he had been watching the house from behind the bush. He broke in while she was vacuuming, so she didn't hear him. It was just a stroke of fate that made her go out as he came in. This man had been known to hurt victims that he found at home when he had committed other crimes.

Thanks to Teema's warning, Faye and little Artie were safe.

The Prowler

We used to laugh and tell my wife's family that prowlers were in more danger around them than they were around the prowlers.

One night my wife's Aunt Polly and Uncle Johnny heard a noise outside their house. Prowlers had been reported in the neighborhood, so Johnny kept his gun loaded and ready in case he needed it for defense.

"Do you think it's the prowler?" Polly asked anxiously.

"Probably," Johnny answered. "I'm going to sneak out the back door and go around the house and see if I can slip up behind him."

"No, that's too dangerous," Polly objected.

"I'll be fine," he told her. "I just need you to stay inside and be quiet until I come back."

Polly nodded her head, and Johnny, gun in hand, slipped quietly out the door into the darkness.

He crept to the first corner of the house and looked around. Nobody was there. He repeated the process until he was at the last corner. The prowler had to be on this side of the house. He put his finger on the trigger, and took a deep breath. His body tensed as he started to ease around and confront the prowler.

Inside the house Polly was worried and tired of waiting. She began to think that maybe something had happened to Johnny since he had been gone longer than she expected him to be. She decided to go out quietly and check on him.

She went out the door and moved silently in the direction Johnny had gone. She saw him ahead and crept up softly behind his back.

Just as his body tensed, she whispered, "Do you see anybody?"

Johnny was so startled that his gun flew up and fired in the air. Footsteps raced from the side of the house and a voice cursed loudly as the prowler bumped into something beside the garage in his hurry to get away.

Johnny let out a stream of curses, too.

"You let him get away!" he shouted at Polly. "I told you to stay inside!

"I got worried," Polly told him.

"I could have shot you!" Johnny pointed out.

The burglar must have thought Johnny could have shot him, too. They never heard him around their house again.

Lonnie E. Brown

By the time the boys got home, they had destroyed the
note and made up their own version to tell their father.

Lonnie E. Brown

Save the Children

One great thing about growing up when and where I did was that nobody harmed children. The prowlers, bootleggers, moon shiners, gamblers, and others who might be on the wrong side of the law all seemed to want to save children from harm.

I can remember hearing of only one case in which a child was molested and murdered back in 1908, supposedly by her own cousin. The man was arrested and put in jail, but the community was so fired up against him that the sheriff moved him to an adjoining county. The men where the little girl had lived were so outraged that they formed a mob and went after him. A guard at the jail, fearing for his own safety, finally handed the prisoner over to the mob. They took him back to the place where the murder had occurred and hanged him in a tree by the road.

His body was later cut down and buried near the spot.

Through the years, people went by that tree and chipped and chopped off pieces for souvenirs! Finally the last piece was taken, and the hanging tree was gone completely.

I must have served as a warning to any others who might have similar ideas, because no other case like that ever happened again.

One man became angry enough to burn the school, but it happened at night when the children were not there.

It was shocking enough that the school was burned, though. Everybody knew who did it and why, but the arsonist (a man named Marvin) and the man who hired him (a man named James) were never arrested and brought to trial. The arsonist confided in some friends and the word filtered through the neighborhood. Nobody had any real evidence, though. Or maybe nobody wanted to take a chance on getting their own property burned.

It was the custom for teachers to board at the home of one of the students because there were no hotels. Mrs. Haskins came to teach in the one-room community school, and she moved into the home of Ann, one of her older students. James had three sons who were about Ann's age or a little older. Mrs. Haskins didn't know that there was bad blood between the families because of some boundary dispute.

Things went smoothly enough for the first few days of school, but trouble soon began to brew. The boys began to pick on Ann, and Mrs. Haskins intervened on Ann's behalf. There had probably been other times when Ann had instigated trouble, but this wasn't one of them and Mrs. Haskins didn't know about anything but this problem. She punished the boys by keeping them after school.

Mrs. Haskins used the only method at her disposal to contact James and explain what had happened. By the time the boys got home, they had destroyed the note and made up their own version to tell their father. They made it look like the teacher had it in for them because she was living at Ann's house. From then on, James had very bad feelings toward Mrs. Haskins. This was a signal to the boys that they didn't have to behave at school or do anything Mrs. Haskins said. She finally had no choice but to expel them for three days because of their disruptive behavior.

This made James furious. He was heard to declare that nobody would go to that school if his boys couldn't go! He contacted the arsonist, made sure that he had an alibi for himself, and the rest is history. The school burned to the ground that night.

School was held in the church for the rest of that year while a new school was built. James enrolled his sons in another school. Mrs. Haskins never knew until after James died several years later that he had the school burned because of her.

Life Lessons and Home Cures

I learned a lot in school and I had good teachers, but I have to give a lot of credit to storytellers for my education.

I learned a home cure from my Aunt Laurie that healed a wound on my leg when I couldn't walk.

I was just a boy when it happened. I wanted a BB gun more than anything at that point, and Mom and Dad finally agreed that I was old enough and responsible enough to have one if I earned the money for it myself.

In the months that followed, I tried every job I could think of. I picked strawberries and blackberries and sold them. I worked at a gas station cleaning up. I made the most money, though, selling garden seeds and flower seeds. Finally I had enough to order my BB gun from the mail order catalog.

After that came the unbearable pain of waiting. Every day I watched for the mailman to come down the road. Our box was across the cornfield from the house, and if the mailman had a package, he'd blow his horn and wait at the box until somebody came and got it. Every day he just brought letters and drove on.

Then one day, he stopped and blew his horn. I knew he had a package and I knew it was my new BB gun. I took off across the cornfield as fast as I could run instead of going around the road. The corn had been cut, and stubbles were sticking up. That wouldn't have mattered if I had been watching where I was going, but all I could think of was that BB gun. I stumped my toe on a rock and fell forward on a stubble. It ripped a hole on my shin and it hurt awful!

Mom and the mailman saw me fall and both ran to help. They got me to the house and the mailman gave me the package. The BB gun

I'd waited for so long would now have to wait a little longer.

Mom cleaned the wound and put salve on it, but the wound began to look infected. Dad took me to the doctor, who cleaned the wound again. He gave Mom something else to rub on it, but nothing helped. The wound was not healing and it hurt too much to walk. My new BB gun lay by my bed unused.

Then Aunt Laurie came for a visit.

"What happened?" she asked.

Mom told her the story and Aunt Laurie looked at my leg.

"Get me a potato and a knife," she instructed Mom.

I was afraid for a minute that she might be thinking of cutting my leg, but she cut the potato instead. Then she scraped an Irish potato into a mush and added salt to make a poultice.

"Just leave that on his leg," she said. "It will heal in no time."

She was absolutely right! It worked! In no time at all, I was up walking and the wound was healing. I watched very carefully when I took my new BB gun out in the fields to try it out! I had learned more than one lesson in all of that!

Daily Life

I especially liked to hear about life in my grandfathers' time. They always had stories to share and I like to pass them on.

I was surprised to learn about work back then in WPA days. For you young people who may not remember or just didn't pay attention in history class, the WPA was the Works Progress Administration. It was established in the spring of 1935 as part of President Franklin D. Roosevelt's New Deal. Its purpose was to provide economic relief by supplying jobs for the working class of people all across the United States during the Depression.

In our county, each able-bodied man was summoned to work for one week repairing public roads because the county had no money for upkeep. Each worker was responsible for bringing his own tools and his own lunch. If for some reason, a man could not perform this duty, he had to hire someone to take his place.

Personally, I was glad that this practice went out before I came along.

I was always interested in the way some people got their water. If there was no suitable spring nearby, people had to get water from wells. Drilling a well involved time and money, so they wanted to get it right the first time. It was common practice to hire a well digger that was called a Water Wizard or a Water Witch, because he doused for water with a forked stick. He held the end of the forks in his hands and walked around. When the end of the stick pointed down, he knew that was where the water would be. Almost every time, there would be water when they dug the well at the location indicated by the stick.

The most fascinating thing to me was the turkey drives. One of my grandfathers raised hundreds of turkeys. He drove them to market just like cattlemen drove herds of cattle. The cattlemen had an advantage, though. They had control over the cattle. On a turkey drive, the turkeys were definitely in charge.

During the day, the men could shoo them along and keep them in line. Night was a different story. When it was time for the turkeys to sleep, they roosted wherever they chose and there was nothing the men could do about it. Usually, they chose trees along the road, so the "turkey drivers" had to set up camp and wait until morning when the turkeys were ready to travel again. My grandfather said this was sometimes the best part, because everybody would sit around and sing or tell stories while the turkeys ruled the roost. They had to limit their singing, though, because it disturbed the turkeys' sleep.

This seemed like more fun than anything else my grandfather did. I told him once that I wish I could have lived in that time in the past. I thought I might have been a good leader. I remember he smiled at me and told me not to worry.

"You could get your chance yet. A lot of people think that everybody in this country tells stories and that turkeys are still in charge," he chuckled.

I had to think about that one for a while.

And I think I'll leave that thought with you!